Something's Fishy at Ash Lake

The Amber and Elliot Mysteries:

The Mad Hacker
Something's Fishy at Ash Lake

Other books by Susan Brown:

Not Yet Summer
Hey, Chicken Man

Other books by Anne Stephenson:

The Mysterious Mr. Moon (General Publishing)
Paper Treasure (General Publishing))

Something's Fishy at Ash Lake

Anne Stephenson   Susan Brown

Cover by
Susan Gardos

Scholastic Canada Ltd.

Scholastic Canada Ltd.
123 Newkirk Road, Richmond Hill, Ontario, Canada L4C 3G5

Scholastic Inc.
730 Broadway, New York, NY 10003, USA

Ashton Scholastic Pty Limited
PO Box 579, Gosford, NSW 2250, Australia

Ashton Scholastic Limited
Private Bag 1, Penrose, Auckland, New Zealand

Scholastic Publications Ltd.
Villiers House, Clarendon Avenue, Leamington Spa, Warwickshire
CV32 5PR UK

Canadian Cataloguing in Publication Data

Brown, Susan
Something's fishy at Ash Lake

ISBN 0-590-74093-8

I. Stephenson, Anne. II. Title.

PS8587.R69S65 1992   jC813'.54   C92-094366-7
PZ7.B76So 1992

6 5 4 3 2 1   Printed in Canada   2 3 4 5 6/9
Manufactured by Webcom Ltd.

Contents

To our parents:
Jack and Isabel Simpson
Norman and Eleanor Bales

1

That Sinking Feeling

Eugene Sharkman, *a.k.a.* Jaws, hitched up his plaid shorts and surveyed the twenty-odd campers scattered around the computer lab. He recognized several of them from his classes at Ash Grove Junior High, including two of his grade seven students, Amber Mitchell and Liz Elliot.

"I'm pleased to see you're enjoying your first afternoon at Eastern Technology's computer camp," he called above the din. "But remember, the next two weeks aren't going to be all fun and games. We start programming tomorrow."

A collective groan rose from the room.

"That's it. I'm out of here." Amber ejected the

game disk from her computer and got up to leave.

"Hang on," Liz stopped her. "I'm about to break my all-time high."

Eyes firmly fixed on the screen, Liz cranked the joy stick through a series of rapid movements. Miniature neon warriors chased each other across a computerized battlefield.

"Rats!" she cried in dismay as her last player tumbled from sight. "Twelve hundred points short!"

Amber grinned. "Gee, that's too bad, Elliot."

"I can tell you're devastated." Liz set the joy stick down and tightened the elastic holding her dark hair in a ponytail. She frowned as her competitors' scores appeared on the screen. One of the other campers was still way ahead.

"What do you think happened to Craig and Jonathan?" asked Amber, glancing at her watch. "I've been watching for them all afternoon."

"Don't worry, they'll show. No one turns down an opportunity like this."

Eastern Technology, one of the biggest computer firms in the country, had awarded the four friends a camp holiday for their part in foiling a ring of computer pirates operating out of Ash Grove Junior High. Craig's father, Robert Nicholson, was one of the company vice-presidents.

"Yeah, you're right. Craig's probably giving Jonathan the royal tour," Amber decided. "That would be just like him."

Liz was busy calling up her scores from other games for comparison. Out of the ten games she'd played so far, she was leading in three.

Amber ran her fingers impatiently through her copper-red curls. "Any time, Elliot."

"I'm ready, I'm ready." Liz shut off her machine and ran to catch up with Amber as she picked her way between campers and computers across the room and out the door.

The camp had been built years ago in the middle of a thick forest of pine. Well-worn dirt paths crisscrossed through the trees, connecting the various buildings and the beach.

The girls walked down towards the water. They could see the vibrant blue of Ash Lake shimmering through the stands of white ash that surrounded the lake and gave it its name.

"I definitely like it here," declared Liz as they stepped from the shade into the full glare of the sun.

"Me too." Amber pulled a tube of sun protector from her pocket and slathered some of it on her nose. "I just wish my freckles would stop dividing and multiplying."

The two girls plowed their way through the soft sand to the water's edge. Tiny pebbles glistened invitingly beneath the surface. Amber bent down and tested the water with her fingers. It felt cool against her skin. "Let's go for a swim," she suggested.

"Didn't you see the sign?"

"What sign?"

"The one that says no unsupervised swimming." Liz pointed to a white board with red lettering affixed to the base of the lifeguard's chair.

"Does it say anything about boating?" Amber asked, her eye on the small flotilla of colourful paddleboats, canoes and sailboats bobbing gently along the dock nearby.

"Nope."

"Then let's go."

Liz hesitated a moment, then followed her friend onto the wooden dock. There were about a dozen paddleboats in all. Amber chose a yellow one and hopped aboard.

"How do you work these things, anyway?" Liz asked as she cautiously climbed onto the seat beside her friend.

"Easy, it's like riding a bike. You just pedal and use this stick to steer." Amber grabbed the rudder in her left hand. "Okay, go!"

The two girls pedalled furiously. The boat lurched forward, then stopped abruptly.

"Stupid thing must be broken," muttered Amber, her face flushed with exertion.

"Perhaps if we untied it . . . "

"Aagh!"

Amber climbed back onto the dock, released the boat from its mooring, and took a flying leap onto the seat beside Liz. "Okay. Now we're ready." They started pedalling again.

"Just like riding a bike, is it?" Liz demanded several minutes later. "Four metres and three crashed boats. I think we need training wheels."

"Don't worry," Amber reassured her, "I've got the hang of it now." She swung the rudder to the right, narrowly missing another sailboat.

Liz giggled and pedalled harder. They zigzagged past the roped off swimming area and headed for open water.

It was definitely cooler out on the lake. They stopped pedalling and put their feet up on the fibreglass prow. Amber closed her eyes and let the boat drift idly.

"This is the life," sighed Liz.

"You said it," agreed Amber. "No parents, no brothers, and no one to bother us."

"Then what's that noise? Sounds like somebody crying away in the distance."

"Probably a loon or something."

Liz shielded her eyes from the late afternoon sun and peered out across the sparkling lake. She could see a canoe about half a kilometre away, with two very familiar paddlers wearing bright orange and yellow life jackets.

"Hey, look! We've got company. It's Craig and Jonathan, and they're acting very strange."

Amber opened her eyes and sat up. The two

boys had raised their paddles and were gesturing wildly.

"I didn't think they'd be *that* glad to see us here," she commented. "They're even turning around."

Sure enough, the canoe had swung about and was heading towards them. Jonathan Weiss, straight up as usual, sat in the prow of the boat, with Craig Nicholson providing the muscle behind him.

"There's a white thing in the water up ahead. Do you think that could be what they're yelling about?" Liz pointed to a white plastic cone bobbing in the water a few metres away.

"It's just a marker," answered Amber. "Probably some underwater rocks there. We'll steer around it." She moved the rudder to the right and they began pedalling in a wide arc around the buoy.

"Amber, look out!"

Jagged rocks suddenly loomed beneath the surface just ahead of them. Amber viciously cranked the rudder.

"The brakes! Put on the brakes!"

"What brakes? Boats don't have brakes."

Crunch!

The fibreglass hull dragged slowly across the ragged submerged rocks. The boat lurched, came to a momentary stop, then gently drifted free.

Liz cleared her throat. "I think we have a problem."

"No kidding." Amber watched as the water slowly rose up the soles of her sneakers. "I have this sinking feeling we're about to go down with the ship."

"That's not funny," snapped Liz. "We've only been at this camp two hours and twenty-five minutes, and already we're in trouble."

"Some people might say that's an improvement," Amber retorted hotly.

They looked down at the water seeping in, looked up at each other, and then burst out laughing.

"Do you remember the time Lindsay Watson said she'd give you a quarter if you spit on Jane Dobbs's shoes?" Liz chuckled.

"Yeah," Amber said wistfully. "It was the high point of my primary school career." She laughed. "I've never seen old Dobbsie so mad. She's such a snot-nose."

"I'm just glad she's not here to see this," said Liz. "She'd be on our case about it the whole vacation."

"Don't you think there's something fishy about this?" Amber swung her arm in the direction of the plastic cone. "The marker is over there, but the rocks are here."

Liz shrugged. "Maybe it drifted loose. Maybe —"

"Ahoy there!" shouted Craig. "Having a little trouble?"

The boys were about seven metres away now. The sun had bleached Craig's hair a pale blond, and even dark-haired Jonathan had acquired a slight tan since school.

"The dynamic duo strikes again," called Jonathan.

"Yeah, a rock!" snickered Craig.

"You could have warned us," Amber told them.

"What did you think we were waving and yelling for?" asked Jonathan, pulling his paddle from the water.

Amber stared down at her wet sneakers. Liz focussed on the far shoreline.

"You know what I think, Jonathan," Craig said mischievously. "I think that they think that we like them."

"Listen, you idiot! While you're having your little joke, we're taking on water!"

"If we don't get to shore in a hurry," added Liz, "we're going to sink."

"You *can* swim, can't you?"

"Of course we can swim," said Amber through clenched braces. "Come on, Elliot, let's head for the dock."

"You guys don't have a bailing can, do you?" Liz asked calmly.

"*Elliot!*"

"Just thought I'd ask."

Amber turned the rudder and the girls began to pedal again, steering a wide, erratic course around the rocks. The water in the boat had risen past their ankles. It was becoming harder and harder to pedal.

"This'll be the shortest camp holiday on record," huffed Liz. "I don't think my allowance will cover a boat."

"Then pedal harder! If this thing sinks, we might as well pack up and head for home."

The boys drew alongside in their canoe.

"Camp just wouldn't be the same without you," observed Craig. "Better, maybe."

Both boys laughed. The girls stopped pedalling and glared at them.

"Still, the boat's worth saving," added Jonathan. "We'd better tow them to shore."

The boys maneuvered in front of the labouring boat. Craig grabbed the mooring line and tied it to the stern of the canoe.

"You two keep pedalling and we'll paddle," he instructed.

At first they barely moved. Then as they gained momentum, the paddleboat wallowed after the green canoe.

"This is humiliating," muttered Liz.

They had almost made it to shore when a young woman dressed in the camp T-shirt, khaki shorts, and a baseball cap walked onto the beach.

She paused for a moment, staring out at the two boats and their occupants, then strode out onto the dock.

"Oh, no," groaned Liz. "Who's that?"

"Kelly Slemko, the athletic director," said Craig.

"Is that good or bad?" asked Amber.

Jonathan shrugged. "She seemed okay to me."

"What's going on here?" demanded the director as the paddleboat bumped gently into the dock.

"We, uh, hit a rock," Liz confessed. "Craig and Jonathan helped us in."

"Are you all right?"

The girls nodded. "Shouldn't those rocks be marked though?" asked Amber. "We could have really run into trouble."

Kelly stared down at her in surprise. "All the dangerous rocks in the lake are marked."

"Those ones weren't."

"That's ridiculous. I checked them only yesterday." The athletic director looked at Craig and Jonathan for verification.

"Amber's right," Jonathan told her as he and Craig put up their paddles and clambered onto the dock. "The buoys are all out of position."

"We tried to warn them," said Craig.

Kelly Slemko turned back to Amber and Liz. "Jonathan and Craig asked my permission to take out the canoe," she said slowly. "But I don't remember giving it to you two."

"We, uh, didn't know we needed permission," offered Liz.

"Haven't you read the camp handbook yet?"

"We just got here," Amber protested.

"We were going to get to it tonight . . . " Liz faltered.

"What are your names, and what cabins are you in?"

"Amber Mitchell, Cabin Three."

"Liz Elliot, Cabin Three, too."

"Well, Amber and Liz, when you have read the handbook you'll know that no boats are to be taken out without permission." Kelly paused and looked each of them in the eyes in turn. "And especially without life jackets."

"Oh."

Amber opened her mouth to protest, but thought better of it. The athletic director was right. Going without life jackets had been dumb.

The paddleboat was now almost completely immersed. Kelly pursed her lips. "Just get this boat out of the lake before it sinks, girls. And for your sakes, I hope that crack in the hull can be fixed." Then she turned and left the dock, heading up the path through the trees.

"I'd feel better if she had yelled at us," said Liz.

"Me, too." Amber stood up, water sloshing

around her legs. "These boats probably cost a lot of money."

The two girls slipped over the side into the waist-high water. With the boys pulling on the paddleboat's mooring line, they managed to push it out of the water and up onto the beach.

Jonathan prodded the hull of the damaged boat with his foot. "It's not that bad. Fibreglass can be patched and repainted. Shouldn't cost too much."

"I hope not," Craig said. "My dad told me if the camp doesn't at least break even this year, the company might have to sell it." He bent down and fingered the jagged edge of the crack.

"But that's crazy," interjected Amber. "The camp's part of Eastern Technology's educational program."

"They still have to make money," Jonathan pointed out.

Liz pulled off her wet sneakers and tossed them onto the beach. "They wouldn't cancel our two free weeks, would they?" Jonathan put his arm around her reassuringly. "I'm sure that as long as the vice-president of finance doesn't know about you two, it'll be okay, won't it, Craig?"

"Maybe if I put in a good word for them," drawled Craig. He straightened up just as Amber's water-logged sneaker flew across the prow of the paddleboat.

"I think it's time to go, Craig," advised Jonathan.

"Yeah, it must be almost dinnertime." Craig gave the girls a last salute, then the two boys trotted across the beach in the direction of the cabins, leaving the girls fuming in their wake.

"Those guys really make me burn," Amber grunted as she and Liz heaved the boat over. The water sloshed out and made brown sugar patterns before it disappeared into the sand.

Liz leaned against the hull of the overturned boat and stared after the boys. "I think someone should take the wind out of their sails, don't you, Amber?"

"I couldn't agree with you more."

Amber retrieved her sneaker, and the two girls picked their way carefully back to camp in their bare feet.

2

Things That Go
Bump in the Night

By the time Amber and Liz got back to their cabin, all the other bunks had been taken. Knapsacks and sleeping bags lay every which way around the deserted room. The girls quickly changed their wet shorts and socks, then set out for the dining hall.

"I hope we meet the rest of our cabinmates at dinner," Amber said.

"If they're all as nice as Cathy Daniels, we're laughing."

"Is she the girl whose score you were trying to beat?"

"Yeah. She's really good . . . but I like her anyway," said Liz.

They jogged down the dirt pathway to the clearing where the main wooden camp buildings stood. As they passed the computer lab and arts and crafts room, they noticed a dark-haired man replacing a screen on one of the windows.

"Who's he?"

Liz shrugged. "Probably the camp handyman."

A larger building housed the kitchen, dining hall and camp offices. The fragrant aroma of Italian cooking filled the air around it.

Amber breathed in deeply. "Something sure smells good."

They pounded eagerly up the steps and across the wide cedar porch to join the other campers in the dining room's noisy food line. Their cabin counsellor, Michelle, was just ahead of them.

"Where have you two been?"

"Exploring," said Amber. She sniffed appreciatively and picked up a tray and utensils. "Mmm, I thought camp food was supposed to be awful."

"Not here," said Michelle. "Mrs. Dainty's a fantastic cook."

"Hey, look at this," Liz interjected. "There's whipped cream on everything."

"All right. Calorie city! I love it."

"Tell Mrs. Dainty," Michelle pointed down the line to where a short, very round woman was serving up platefuls of food to the campers ahead of them.

The girl behind Liz leaned forward. "Rumour has it that Mrs. Dainty used to be a cook on a tramp steamer."

"Really?"

The other camper nodded. "She even has a rose tattooed on her arm."

Liz's eyes shot to the front of the line. "Which arm?"

"Left."

"Say when," the cook ordered a moment later as she heaped Liz's plate with lasagna.

But Liz didn't hear a word. She was mesmerized by the red rose tattoo just visible beneath the sleeve on the plump arm in front of her.

Mrs. Dainty paused. "Are you sure you're going to eat this much, dear? You can always come back for seconds."

"No . . . I mean, yes. I was daydreaming," Liz stammered. She'd never seen a woman with a tattoo before.

"The first day is always confusing," Mrs. Dainty smiled. She handed Liz the plate. "Away you go."

Liz nodded, then followed Amber to an empty table. They plunked their trays down and sat on the benches facing each other. Amber took a bite of her garlic bread and surveyed the scene.

"Anybody look familiar?" Liz asked.

Amber shook her head. "Just a few kids I saw this afternoon."

They were halfway through their lasagna when Cathy Daniels showed up. "Can we sit with you?"

"Sure, sit down," Liz said. "Who's we?"

Before Cathy could answer, an immaculate, dark-haired girl slid her tray onto the table.

"Amber, Liz, I'd like you to meet Jane Dobbs," said Cathy. "She's in our cabin."

"Jane!" Amber exclaimed. "What are you doing here?"

"Nice to see you, too, Amber." Jane sat down beside Liz. "Hi, Elliot. How you doing?"

"You're in Cabin Three? With us?" Liz squeaked.

Jane turned to Cathy. "I'm really glad you're here, Cathy. When I found out that Amber and Liz were in my cabin, I was afraid I wouldn't have anyone intelligent to talk to."

Amber sputtered. Liz grabbed her arm. "Save it," she hissed. "Here come the macho twins."

Craig and Jonathan sauntered up to the table.

"Ladies." Craig nodded to Amber and Liz, then leaned on the table facing Jane and Cathy.

"Did the girls tell you about their little episode on the lake this afternoon?"

"They were just about to." Jane locked eyes with Amber.

"It's nothing you'd be interested in," Amber muttered.

"Actually," Jonathan cleared his throat, "we really came over to deliver a message." He paused and looked almost apologetic.

"Well?" prompted Liz.

"Kelly Slemko had to tell the camp director about the boat. He wants to see you after dinner in his office."

Jane delicately tore a piece off her garlic bread and popped it in her mouth. "You two just can't stay out of trouble, can you?"

It was all Amber could do to keep from smearing her lemon meringue pie all over Jane's prissy face.

* * *

They didn't finish eating until the dining room was practically empty.

"I don't think we can put this off much longer, Amber."

Amber wiped the last crumbs of pie from her face and dropped her napkin on the tray. "Okay. Let's go."

They deposited their dishes on the trolley by the kitchen and crossed the hall to the camp offices. *WALTER KINCAID — CAMP DIRECTOR* was stencilled on the frosted glass of the middle door. Amber knocked. No answer. She tried again.

"Now what do we do?" asked Liz when there was no reply.

Amber pushed on the door. It swung open.

"I don't know." She peeked into the room. Nobody was inside. "Hey, look, there's a map of Ash Lake." She pointed across the room.

Liz followed Amber inside. The director's office was sparsely furnished with a metal desk, two chairs and a filing cabinet. A bulletin board with copies of camp schedules and a large calendar hung on one wall.

Directly in front of them, a coloured map of the lake and camp took up the whole wall. Blue pins marked the buildings; red and black pins stuck out in a random pattern across the map.

Amber crossed the room and jabbed her finger under a white pin on the blue lake. "The white pins must be the markers."

"We were right!" exclaimed Liz. She pinpointed the exact spot where they'd run afoul that afternoon. "There should have been a buoy right there."

"Which is the only reason you have not been suspended from this camp!"

The girls whirled around.

A stocky, slightly balding man stared at them from the office door. He wore an Eastern Technology camp T-shirt, and his glasses hung from a string about his neck.

Amber disliked him on sight. "You must be Mr. Kincaid," she said.

"That's right." He strode into the room. "And you're Amber Mitchell and Liz Elliot. May I ask why you are in my office?"

"You sent for us."

"But why are you *in* my office."

"The, uh, door was open and we saw the map . . . " Liz stammered.

"Next time, wait out in the hall."

Amber was tempted to salute, but settled for a mumbled "Yes, sir," instead.

"I've heard about your exploits at Ash Grove Junior High." Kincaid paused. "Just remember, you're at my camp now, and I don't have time for your amateur theatrics."

"But what about the buoy?" persisted Amber. "Shouldn't you find out who moved it?"

"That's my business, not yours." The camp director glared at her, then sniffed loudly. "What's that smell?"

Liz flushed. "Our sneakers. They're still wet."

Kincaid closed his eyes momentarily and shook his head. "Elliot, Elliot, that name sounds familiar!"

"My mother's the mayor of Ash Grove."

"Really?" Kincaid looked at her with interest.

"I wonder what she'd have to say about your behaviour."

Liz stared at him stonily.

"Yes, well, I'll have Bennie take a look at the paddleboat in the morning," said Kincaid. "In the meantime, your boating privileges are withdrawn."

"But — "

"But what?"

Neither girl said anything.

"Then I suggest you join your cabinmates. The campfire is about to begin."

* * *

Kelly Slemko held a match under the dry kindling. A moment later, the campfire blazed and sparked upward into the black sky. The campers, sitting on logs around the bonfire, cheered loudly.

"You've all met your cabin counsellors by now, so for the very few of you who haven't wandered into the computer lab yet, I'd like to introduce our computer director, Mr. Eugene Sharkman! Mr. Sharkman?"

Jaws stepped out of the shadows and into the light of the bonfire. He was wearing a glow-in-the-dark T-shirt. A loud cheer went up.

Kelly continued to make introductions. There were cheers for Mrs. Dainty, but only polite attention and a few subdued hoots for Mr. Kincaid's welcome and rundown of camp rules.

"Each day's schedules will be posted in the morning before breakfast," he told the campers. "With twelve cabins and seventy-two campers, we can't all take part in the same activity at the same time." He paused and looked around the circle of faces. "There are also rules regarding your free time. For instance, there is to be no swimming or boating without permission."

"Could he mean us?" Amber whispered to Liz.

"Shh!"

"The tuck shop," Kincaid went on, "is operated by our own Mrs. Dainty. It will be open every afternoon between two and four. It has a fine selection of healthful snacks." He flashed a rather toothy smile around the campfire. "Are there any questions? . . . Okay, I'll turn the ceremonies back to Kelly and we'll have some fun."

"Fun?" grumbled Amber. "The man doesn't know the meaning of the word."

"It's in the book," Liz told her. "Rule 5, subsection 12 — *Campers must enjoy themselves at all times.*"

The cabin counsellors stepped forward, and for the next forty minutes entertained the campers with skits and a singsong.

"All right, everybody," Kelly called out when the last warble had died down. "A special treat! Hot dogs and marshmallows."

"Okay, Liz." Amber's eyes sparkled in the

firelight. "This is our chance. Everyone will be busy eating."

"Let's go," Liz agreed.

They glanced across the campfire to where Craig and Jonathan were roasting hot dogs with their cabinmates. Silently, Liz and Amber backed away until they were hidden in the deep shadows of the trees that surrounded the clearing.

Cathy Daniels watched them leave. "Now what are they up to?"

"Who knows? They thrive on melodrama," said Jane. Half a moment later, she got up and made her way around the circle to where Craig and Jonathan were sitting with their friends.

* * *

"Sure is dark," Liz whispered, stopping to take stock of their surroundings.

"Oomph," Amber grunted as she banged into the other girl. "Warn me if you stop. I can't see my hand in front of me. This is you, isn't it?"

Liz giggled. "Okay, what's the plan?"

Amber leaned over and whispered in Liz's ear.

"Oh, Amber! That's so rotten — I love it!"

"There's a light in the kitchen. Let's go." Giggling and stumbling, they headed towards the dining hall.

"Is anyone around?" Liz whispered, peering

into the shadows of the dimly lit building. She looked back at the campfire.

"Looks like the kitchen door is open," Amber whispered back. Cautiously, they inched along the side of the building. Amber reached out and tentatively pushed on the screen door.

"It must be latched from the inside," Liz said.

"No problem." Amber pulled a Swiss Army knife from her pocket. "Dad gave it to me," she explained as she opened the blade. "He figures we're in the wilds or something. It even has a can opener — and a corkscrew. I wonder what he thinks I'll use a corkscrew for?"

"Will you hurry up! What if Kincaid walks by?"

"Right." Carefully, Amber slid the thin blade between the door and the frame and lifted the latch. She closed her camp knife and pushed on the door again.

Squeeeeaak!

Liz shivered involuntarily.

The steel counters and commercial appliances gleamed in the light of the overhead kitchen lamp. "The fridge," Amber whispered, and pointed.

They hurried to the huge double refrigerator at the far end of the kitchen and yanked it open.

"There's enough here to feed an army," Liz said.

"Yes, but where's the whipped cream?"

"There, behind the lettuce." Liz lifted out one of several aerosol cans.

"Great." Amber shut the door and they turned to go.

"*Amber!*" Liz clutched her friend's arm. "Did you hear something?"

They stood perfectly still, ears straining, hearts thumping in the darkness. Suddenly, a harsh scrape came from the direction of Kincaid's office.

"It's Kincaid!" Liz squeaked. "We've got to hide."

"Quick, over there!" Amber pointed to a work table against the wall. They dove under and crouched in the shadows.

Several minutes dragged by. Then, "Amber," whispered Liz, "Kincaid was still at the campfire when we left. How could he have gotten here before us?"

Amber frowned. "Who's in his office then?"

"I don't know, and I don't care."

"Elliot! What kind of an attitude is that?"

"I call it my survivor instinct."

"Come on, let's go." Amber began to crawl out from under the table.

"Wait!" Liz grabbed Amber's shorts and hauled her back.

"Do you mind?"

"Ssh!"

A shadow slipped across the floor. Soft

footsteps sounded from the far side of the kitchen. The two girls cowered against the wall. They could see feet, then legs. Moonlight silhouetted a dark figure by the door.

Squeeeeeaaak!

The prowler cursed softly as he slipped outside.

The girls' breath came in quiet gasps. "Let's get out of here," Amber whispered finally. They crawled out from under the table and headed for the door.

Squeeeeeaaak! Bang!

Amber and Liz dove into the concealing shadows and leaned, panting, against a tree.

"Who do you think that was?"

"I don't know," said Liz, clutching the whipped cream container tightly. "But whoever it was didn't want to be seen."

The two girls stumbled through the trees, tripping over roots and snagging their shirts on branches.

"Revenge shouldn't be this difficult," Liz grumbled. "Which cabin did you say they're in?"

Amber stopped and turned around. "I thought you knew."

"Great!" said Liz. "We go to all this trouble, and we don't even know what cabin they're in?"

"Yoohoo! Amber! Liz! Come out, come out wherever you are."

"Aagh!" Amber slumped against a tree. "I

don't believe this. We're losing our touch."

Craig and Jonathan appeared in the moonlight. Liz thrust the can of whipped cream behind her back.

"When we heard you'd left the campfire, it wasn't hard to figure out you were up to something," Craig told them. "So after a couple more hot dogs, we decided to investigate."

"Good thing, too," Jonathan drawled, "or you might be wandering around half the night looking for us."

"I'd rather meet Bigfoot."

The next second, a branch cracked loudly in the brush beside them. Then a powerful flashlight snapped on, trapping their faces in a blinding beam.

"Hey!" Craig shouted. "Turn that off!" He made a grab for the light. Too late. The beam disappeared. Heavy footsteps crashed away through the brush.

Jonathan whistled softly. "What was all that about?"

None of them had the faintest idea.

As they headed back towards camp, the sound of a motorboat starting up drifted through the night air.

3

Out on a Limb

The morning sun filtered through the leaves of the ash tree, casting a dappled pattern on the ground below. Amber shifted her weight and peered down at the deserted campsite.

"What time is it?" she whispered.

Liz checked her watch. "Nine forty-five. Cabin Seven should be finished helping in the kitchen any minute."

Amber patted the plastic bag full of water balloons. "Whoever said 'revenge is sweet' knew what they were talking about."

Liz giggled. "I can't wait to drop one right on Craig's head. Three days of his smart cracks are all I can take."

"Just don't hit Irwin by mistake."

"And cut off our candy supply? No way."

Irwin Dexter, Craig and Jonathan's slightly overweight cabinmate, had a stash of chocolate bars under his bunk which he was willing to share — for a price.

"I wonder why the tuck shop only sells health food?" Liz puzzled. "If word of this gets out, no kid in their right mind will come to this camp."

"They're not going to come anyway, when they hear about kitchen detail."

The screen door of the dining hall slapped shut.

"Sssh!" warned Liz. "Someone's coming."

"Good. One of these balloons is starting to leak." A tiny stream of water had escaped and was forming a pool beside Amber's leg.

"Oh, no! It's Weird Walter!"

The camp director strode into the clearing below, clipboard in hand.

"What's he doing, Amber?"

"The box step, I think."

Kincaid was taking long strides across the clearing, first one way, then another. At each turn he made a notation on his clipboard.

"No wonder they call him Weird Walter," whispered Amber.

"Be quiet," pleaded Liz. "He's coming this way."

Kincaid paced out the distance to their tree,

stopped directly beneath them and took off his baseball cap. He was so close, Liz could practically count the thin red hairs on the top of his head. He added more figures to the notes on his clipboard, drew several rectangles, then studied them. From where Liz sat, it looked like a map of the campsite, only the buildings were in the wrong places.

She glanced at Amber to see what she made of the notes, but Amber was staring, fascinated, as a rivulet of water etched a path down her leg — on a direct course for Kincaid's head!

The drop at the bottom got bigger and bigger. For a few agonizing seconds it hung in the air.

·And then . . . *splat!*

Kincaid's hand shot up and slapped the wet spot. "Darn birds," he muttered, putting his hat back in place.

Liz held her breath. Amber clamped her free hand over her mouth and clung shaking to the tree. The water dripped slowly down the trunk. Finally, Kincaid finished writing on the clipboard and headed towards his office on the far side of the dining hall.

"Can you believe that?" Liz collapsed back against the tree trunk.

"Too bad it wasn't really a bird," Amber said. "A giant bald eagle — with diarrhea!"

"Amber, that's gross. Hey, here come the guys!"

Cabin Seven clomped down the steps of the dining hall past Kincaid and started across the clearing towards the computer lab.

"Okay, partner," whispered Amber. "Do your stuff." She passed over two full balloons.

"Hey, Craig! Jonathan!" called Liz. "We need your help."

The boys looked around.

"Where are you?" yelled Craig.

"Up here," said Liz plaintively. "In the ash tree. I'm stuck . . . "

The two boys broke away from their cabin-mates and headed towards Liz's voice.

"Is Amber with you?" Jonathan asked suspiciously.

Amber winked at Liz. "I've twisted my ankle," she wailed.

The boys came closer.

"The suckers," Amber whispered.

"If we rescue you again," bargained Craig, "you have to take our next kitchen detail."

"And do our laundry on Saturday," added Jonathan. He stopped, beneath the tree, arms folded over his chest.

"Over my dead body!" screamed Amber. She swung a balloon from behind her back and let fly. *"Hiiy ya!"*

The first balloon burst on Jonathan's head. The second one landed in the dirt at his feet, splattering mud everywhere. Craig caught his in the face. Liz's second balloon burst on his shoulder.

"We'll get you, you turkeys!" he spluttered, scrubbing at his face.

But Amber and Liz had already swung down from the tree and were running as fast as they could for the computer lab.

* * *

"Good morning, girls," Mr. Sharkman said as the two girls slipped breathlessly into the computer room. He was in his element, surrounded by an array of humming electronic equipment. Campers in Eastern Technology T-shirts were chatting and busily keying in their computer projects.

"Find yourself a place," he instructed the late arrivals.

Amber and Liz sat down on either side of Cathy. "Did we miss anything?"

Cathy shook her head. "No. Where are Craig and Jonathan? They didn't come in with the rest of the guys from Cabin Seven. I've written a program even Jonathan can't crack."

"I think they'll be a little late," said Liz. "They had to go back to their cabin for some dry clothes."

Cathy eyed her cabinmate. "Accident in the kitchen?"

"Not exactly." Amber reached for the power

switch. "It was more like an ambush. Hey, what's wrong with this computer?"

The room went deadly silent as one by one the campers realized everything had shut down.

"Don't panic, anyone," said Mr. Sharkman. "It's probably just a power failure."

"Everything was fine until Liz and Amber showed up," muttered Jane to the boy beside her.

"Just stay where you are and I'll investigate." No sooner had Jaws started across the room than Craig and Jonathan burst through the doorway.

"Mr. Sharkman," Craig yelled. "The generator!"

"It's on fire," gasped Jonathan.

Jaws took a quick look around. "Jonathan, the fire extinguisher! Craig, inform Mr. Kincaid! The rest of you, head for the beach."

The main generator was in a shed midway between the computer lab and the dining hall. By the time Mr. Sharkman and Jonathan reached the building, smoke billowed from its only window.

"Stand back, son. I'll have to kick the door in. It's padlocked."

Mr. Sharkman took aim and let fly. With a resounding crack, the door swung open, leaving the rusty lock swinging on its hasp. Grabbing the fire extinguisher from Jonathan, Mr. Sharkman swiftly entered the shed and doused the smoking generator with foam.

"Well, this is great, just great," grumbled Mr. Kincaid from the doorway. "I just had that thing fixed last week."

Jaws glanced up at him sharply. "You should be thankful no one got hurt."

"Naturally."

"Sir?" Jonathan stepped through the doorway. "What's this?" He poked at some charred remnants lying near the generator. "Probably an old rag or something," Kincaid said. "I'll speak to Bennie about it."

"Mr. Sharkman, couldn't a spark from the generator set an oily rag on fire?"

"Absolutely." Jaws turned to face the camp director. "Dangerously sloppy on someone's part, wouldn't you say?"

* * *

"I feel like Cinderella," Liz muttered as she scraped the lunch plates and handed them to Amber for washing. "Before the ball."

"Too bad we can't turn Weird Walter into a pumpkin," Cathy Daniels said as she pushed another trolley full of dirty dishes over to Amber.

"He's already a rat," declared Amber.

"Now, girls," Mrs. Dainty admonished. "We all have to pitch in, but at least the generator will be fixed this afternoon and we can use the dishwasher again." She sprinkled more flour onto the worktable and deftly began rolling out pie pastry.

"My cousin came here last year, and no one did kitchen work," said Annette Marini. She held up her hands in dismay. "Just look at my nails! They're all chipped."

"Annette's right," added Brenda Chang. "My parents spent a lot of money to send me here. They didn't expect I'd have to work for my keep."

Mrs. Dainty shrugged. "This is a valuable piece of land, so close to Ash Grove. It takes a lot of money to run a business . . . " She sighed. "I know. My husband and I used to own a marina."

"What happened?" asked Amber.

"A resort chain bought up our mortgage and forced us out."

"How did they do that?" Brenda stopped drying dishes to listen.

"They demanded we pay back every cent we'd borrowed to buy the marina within thirty days. When we couldn't raise the money, the marina became their property."

"But that's not fair!" exclaimed Brenda.

"I know, honey, but that's life."

"Isn't there anything you can do?" asked Amber.

"No. That's why I'm working here." Mrs. Dainty picked up a paring knife and trimmed the edge of the pastry.

"Even so, Kincaid should get you more kitchen help," Liz said. "Which reminds me, where's Jane?" asked Amber.

Liz shrugged her shoulders. "She knew we had kitchen detail, all right. I saw her check the schedule."

Amber called to her other cabinmates. "Does anybody know where Jane is?"

"She was at lunch," Brenda answered. "But I don't know where she went after that."

"I do," said Annette. "She went down to the general store to pick up the mail for Mr. Kincaid. I think she wants to get some candy so she can go into competition with Irwin."

"This I've got to see," Amber said, shaking her head. "Old Dobbsie getting into the black market . . ."

* * *

Liz flopped down on the bottom bunk later that afternoon and groaned. "I'm so stiff I can hardly move."

"You're just out of shape," Amber said. Her bare legs were dangling down from the upper bunk where she sat eating a bag of unsalted peanuts from the tuck shop. "Another few days and you'll be as hard as a rock."

"Don't mention rocks. Hitting that rock with the paddleboat the first day was a big mistake. Kincaid's been watching us ever since."

"Yeah, but at least we've got our boating privileges back. You know, Elliot," Amber said between chews, "I've been thinking — "

"Oh, no, you don't. Whenever you start to think, we get into trouble."

"Very funny." Amber slid down and sat on the edge of Liz's bed.

"Okay, everybody, up and at 'em!" Michelle strode into the cabin, whistle around her neck. "We've been challenged to a volleyball match before dinner."

"Who're we playing today?" asked Cathy. She looked up from her book.

"Cabin Seven," replied Michelle.

"Great!" Annette perked up immediately. "Aren't they the cute guys we have computer lab with?"

"Depends on what you consider cute," muttered Amber. "Craig and Jonathan are in that cabin."

"And they play to win," warned Liz.

"That's the whole point," Michelle said.

"Well, I think there's too much emphasis on competition," Jane complained from her bunk. "It's how you play the game that counts."

"That's just because you fouled the ball and lost the game for us yesterday when we were playing the girls from Cabin Two," Amber said scornfully.

"Will you two can it?" Michelle picked up Jane's sneakers and tossed them at her. "Come on. I've got a reputation to protect."

"But I'm exhausted," grumbled Jane. "All

this swimming and volleyball and stuff is wearing me out — not to mention kitchen duty."

"What kitchen duty?" demanded Amber. "You were off running errands for Kincaid after lunch today. We were the ones doing all the work."

"Why should I waste my talents on menial labour when you're so obviously better suited?" Jane taunted.

Amber grabbed Liz's pillow and winged it across the room. The rest of the girls followed her lead, burying Jane beneath a pile of feathers.

"Save your energy for tomorrow," advised Michelle. "That's when you're really going to get a workout."

"Tomorrow? What's tomorrow?" Liz asked.

"Tomorrow," Michelle explained, "is the Great Race."

4

The Great Race

"All right," called Kelly Slemko to the twelve campers and two counsellors gathered around the flagpole. "You're here to take part in Ash Lake's version of the Triathlon."

Cabin Three and Cabin Seven answered her announcement with ragged shouts and cheers.

"The Great Race is divided into three parts," Kelly continued. "The first part is to see how fast you can pack and load your gear into your assigned canoes. The second part is the actual race to Skull Island."

"Skull Island?" Irwin asked. "Which one is that?"

"The biggest one in the lake," replied Kelly.

"It's a little more than two kilometres straight out from the dock."

"You mean we have to paddle a loaded canoe for two kilometres?" Irwin demanded. His cheeks reddened alarmingly.

"Oh, Irwin," Jane trilled, "you can use the exercise. No one will think less of you when you lose."

Irwin drew himself up. "I never lose," he told her.

"Right!" Jonathan agreed.

"Way to go, Irwin." Craig thumped him on the back. "Let's hear it for Cabin Seven!"

"The third part of the race," interrupted Kelly loudly, "is setting up camp. The first cabin to complete all three parts wins the Triathlon."

"What's the prize?" Cathy asked.

"The prize," announced Kelly, "is a double layer chocolate fudge cake baked by Mrs. Dainty."

"I will have died and gone to heaven," Liz declared.

"You're not the only one who thinks so," Amber laughed. "Look at Irwin."

Craig and Jonathan were valiantly supporting their cabinmate, who appeared to have fainted with ecstasy.

"And just to add to the challenge," Kelly yelled to get their attention, "the losing cabin has to cook dinner!"

"We'd better lose, then," called out Michelle. "Those guys will poison us!"

"Oh, yeah?" answered Rick, the counsellor for Cabin Seven. "We can cook better than anyone, right, guys?"

The boys backed him up loudly.

"All right, all right," Kelly brought the group to order. She held up her stopwatch. "Any more questions? No? Okay. On your mark. Get set! *Go!*"

There was a mad stampede as campers flew in all directions.

"What am I going to wear?" screamed Annette Marini as the girls raced for their cabin.

"Who cares?" hollered Michelle. "Those boys won't even pack clean socks! Just grab your toothbrush and some clean underwear. And don't forget those life jackets!"

They burst into the cabin, grabbed their knapsacks, and began stuffing them with everything in sight.

"I'm ready," called Liz. She fastened her life jacket and headed for the door. "Let's go get 'em."

Amber dashed after her. Jane, Cathy and Brenda were right behind. Michelle's stuff was all ready to go — this was her second Triathlon of the summer.

"Has anybody seen my blow dryer?"

"*Annette!*" the girls yelled in chorus.

"Calm down," cautioned Michelle. "We'll

never win if we panic." She walked over to Annette's bunk and put her hand on the girl's shoulder.

"Annette, there is no electricity where we are going. There are no flush toilets, and there's no running water. Now, *move it!*" she shrieked. "We're going to beat those boys, with or without lipstick!"

They tore out of the cabin and headed for the dock, knapsacks and sleeping bags flying.

Cabin Seven was pounding down a parallel path, Craig and Jonathan in the lead. Kelly stood waiting on the dock, stopwatch in hand, braced for the inevitable collision.

"Come on, come on," puffed Michelle. "Head for the canoes on the right!"

The two sets of campers crashed onto the dock like a herd of moose.

"Get out of my way!" screamed Brenda. Two of the boys ducked as she made a beeline for one canoe.

"Hey, watch it!" yelled Craig. Too late. Liz's backpack clipped him on the ear as she swung it off her back.

"Sorry about that."

"Grrr!"

"Hit the deck, girls! Here comes Irwin!"

The campers scrambled into canoes as Irwin lumbered onto the dock. He was laden down with a bulging knapsack and sleeping bag, and clutched a duffle bag protectively to his chest.

"Irwin," Rick pleaded, "it's only for one night."

"But, Rick," he panted, "what a business opportunity! Fifteen people stranded on an island with no convenience stores anywhere . . . "

"Irwin, get in your canoe!" shouted Jonathan. "The girls are almost loaded up."

"Too late!" Kelly clicked her stopwatch with authority. "The first round goes to Cabin Three."

"*All right!*" The girls shouted in triumph.

"Don't worry, guys," yelled Craig. "With Amber and Liz together in one boat, we'll win the next round for sure!"

"Just make sure they're not carrying the chocolate cake," called Jonathan. "It'll go down with the ship!"

"Don't worry," interrupted Kelly before war could break out. "The cake goes in the motorboat with me."

"Now for the second part of the Triathlon — the race to Skull Island. The first team to reach the island with all three canoes wins the race. Counsellors, untie your lines."

Quickly, Rick and Michelle untied the canoes from the dock and returned to their positions as passengers. The campers were ready, paddles in hand, for Kelly to start the race.

"On your mark. Get set! *Go!*"

The water churned as a dozen paddles dug into Ash Lake.

"Paddle together! You're supposed to be a team!" hollered Michelle as Cabin Three's lead canoe jerked forward in one direction, then another.

"We're trying! We're trying!" But the harder Amber and Liz paddled, the more they swerved and wobbled. One by one the other canoes pulled ahead.

"See you later!" Craig called over his shoulder.

"Come on, Elliot," urged Amber. "We're out of sync."

"Okay . . . stroke on the count of three," Liz puffed. "One, two, THREE! One, two, THREE!"

"Finally," Amber grunted as their canoe began to gather speed.

The six canoes shot across the water toward Skull Island. Even with Rick in their canoe, Craig and Jonathan were way out in front. Cathy and Jane were close behind, followed by the other campers. Liz and Amber stroked in hot pursuit.

"Faster, Liz! We're almost up to Irwin's canoe!"

"I can't! My arms feel like they're falling off."

"But we're gaining on them!"

Irwin looked back. His pudgy arms moved faster. Liz groaned and dug her paddle deeper into the water. The gap between Amber and Liz and the other campers narrowed.

"Faster," panted Amber. "We still have a chance!"

They pulled ahead of Irwin and his partner, then passed Brenda and Annette, who had Michelle kneeling in the centre of their canoe. "Way to go!" she cheered as they went by. "You can do it!"

Amber and Liz paddled even harder. They nosed ahead of the other two canoes and fixed their sights on Craig and Jonathan. The lead canoe was about three hundred metres from Skull Island.

"We're catching up!"

The added weight of their counsellor seemed to be slowing Craig and Jonathan down. Their lead had been whittled down to about four canoe lengths.

"Stroke! Stroke!" urged Rick. Craig's paddle smacked the water awkwardly and he lost his rhythm.

Three lengths and closing. The boys paddled madly. The two canoes were neck and neck with only fifty metres to the island!

Amber sliced furiously at the water with her paddle.

Crack! The blade smacked into a submerged rock and snapped in half!

The boys pulled ahead.

"Keep paddling," Liz gasped. "The team can still win."

But Amber's paddle barely made a ripple in the water. One by one, the others passed them. By the time the girls limped into the bay at Skull Island, everyone else had already beached their crafts.

"Of all the dirty, rotten things to happen!" Amber growled.

"Tough luck," called Jonathan. "You were really close."

"I'm beginning to think you guys are jinxed," Craig said as he tied their line to a tree.

"You'd think they could at least paddle a canoe without a disaster," muttered Jane.

"I didn't see you offering any help," Amber retorted, gently swinging the broken shaft of her paddle.

Jane glared back at her.

"Now don't give up, girls." Kelly had watched the tail end of the race from the island. "Each team has won one event. We still have the tiebreaker."

"Yeah, lighten up, Amber," said Liz, poking her best friend. "We'll get ours back. The Triathlon's not over yet."

"Here's the plan," announced Kelly. "Not too far down that path," she turned and pointed to a well-travelled dirt trail leading into the woods, "you'll come to a clearing. On either side of the campsite you'll find a canvas bag containing a tent. The first team to set up camp, tent flaps up and sleeping bags rolled out, wins!"

"No problem, right, guys?" Rick looked at his charges with confidence.

"Excuse me, but does this tent have bathroom facilities?"

"*Irwin!*"

"Just curious," Irwin defended himself.

"You'll find the facilities about thirty metres beyond the campsite," answered Kelly. "Downwind."

"Is there a His and Hers?" asked Annette.

"Two-seaters?" asked another camper.

"Come on," Craig put in, "Irwin's not that fat."

"I'm selling toilet paper at two cents a sheet," announced Irwin.

"*Irwin!*"

"It's designer toilet paper. Scented even!"

"All right, all ready." Kelly raised her stopwatch to signal the start of the race. "Now, remember, you're on your own for this. Your counsellors can only offer suggestions. On your mark. Get set! *Go!*"

The campers grabbed their gear and scrambled up the path. Irwin brought up the rear, still clutching his duffle bag. As the kids burst into the clearing, each team raced to a tent and began tugging at the canvas bag.

"No fair. Ours has a knot."

"What's all this rope for?"

Within a few minutes Cabin Three had rolled their tent out on the ground.

"It's huge!" Brenda eyed the canvas uncertainly. "Where do we start?"

"You four pull out the corners," instructed Michelle. "Jane, you and Amber go get the poles."

"Oh, oh," muttered Liz under her breath to Cathy. "Here comes trouble."

"Hurry and get the longest pole in the centre of the tent."

"Right," said Amber. She bent down to pick it up.

"Don't bother," snapped Jane. "I've got it." She slid the pole out of Amber's reach and jogged to the tent.

Fuming, Amber followed. Without a word, she lifted the canvas for Jane to position the supporting pole.

"Good, now get the rest of the poles," Jane commanded.

"Yes, ma'am," Amber grumbled, but she ran for the poles and helped Jane put them up.

"The rest of you get those pegs ready," coached Michelle. "The boys are getting ahead of us. Somebody get the mallet."

Amber and Jane both raced for the mallet.

"I've got it this time," hissed Amber. "Give it to me!"

"No." Jane stood there holding the mallet defiantly.

"Girls, the race!" Michelle yelled.

"I don't believe this!" wailed Liz. "Of all the times for you two to fight."

"Come on, you guys!" shouted Cathy. "You can fight later."

"She's right," Amber admitted. "Let's go." After a split-second battle of wills, she and Jane went together to each corner and hammered in the pegs.

"We have six pegs left over," Annette said.

"Forget it," panted Brenda, still holding her corner out until it could be tied. "They always put in extras."

Liz and Cathy looped the ropes around the pegs and pulled the guy lines taut. The other girls raced to roll up the tent flaps and get their gear inside.

"Lay everything out neatly," cautioned Michelle, "or you'll be disqualified."

The girls swarmed inside the tent and were out again in a flash.

"We're done! We're done!" called Michelle.

"So are we!" cried Rick from the other side of the clearing.

"Then it's a tie," Kelly decided.

"That's a cop-out!" yelled one of the boys.

"Inspection! Inspection!" began the chant from Cabin Seven. All the campers joined in until Kelly blew her whistle.

"Okay, okay! The team with the neatest sleeping arrangements wins."

The girls looked at each other smugly. "It's in the bag now," said Cathy.

"That's right," Annette agreed. "Boys are pigs."

Kelly strode across the clearing to the girls' tent. She unzipped the mosquito netting and stepped inside. The tent swayed as though being rocked by a rising wind.

Spellbound, the campers watched as the tent collapsed into a billowing heap around the athletic director.

"Hey, girls," called Craig. "What's cooking?"

5

The Ghosts of
Skull Island

Eeeeaayah!

The inhuman scream pierced the laughing chatter around the campfire. Then . . . silence. The campers looked at each other. The shadows seemed to crowd closer to the roaring flames.

"I don't think I like this," Liz whispered. She looked over her shoulder anxiously. "Do you think there are any wild animals out here?"

A few of the campers began to giggle.

"Relax," Amber said.

Eeeaayah!

This time Amber jumped as the scream sounded even louder.

"I think that was closer," Brenda murmured.

Amber grinned nervously. "It's just a gag. They always do this kind of stuff at a campout."

"I can't imagine why," Jane snapped. "I think it's juvenile." She quickly glanced toward the dark trees.

"It's Weird Walter's pet werewolf," Craig offered in a stage whisper. "He's in pain. We gave him our leftovers."

"Very funny."

A bent figure, dressed in rags but gleaming ghostly white, shuffled out of the night towards the campfire.

"Beware . . . beware . . . beware . . . "

"Who's that?" Liz demanded.

Amber stared, wide-eyed, then started to laugh. "It's Kelly. Now I know why she brought that bag of flour when we already had pancake mix packed."

"Kelly?" the figure howled. "Kelly has crossed over to the world beyond. I am the spirit of Skull Island!"

"Give me a break," called Irwin.

"Disbeliever!" She pointed a white finger at him. "I will tell you the story of this terrible place, and then see if you mock me.

"Once, many moons ago, before the white men came, a tribe of Indians lived on the far shore. The chief had two beautiful daughters — beautiful but curious. One night, evil spirits flashed lights across this island. The two princesses stole their father's canoe and paddled towards the lights.

"Later in the night, the tribe was awakened by two terrible screams. In the morning the warriors went to the island and found the chief's canoe, but no princesses — only two skulls, one facing the sunrise, one the sunset.

"The two princesses were never found. Their ghosts have been seen many times, walking and calling to be rescued."

"Yuck," Liz whispered.

"Wait. There's more!" The white figure pivoted, slowly pointing to each of the campers. "Ever since that day, each of the tribe's young people has had to spend at least one night alone on the island. If he or she was brave and pure of heart, they lived. If not . . . if not . . . " The figure looked around slowly. "If not . . . then two extra work details back at camp."

"Augh!" Irwin shouted. The other campers began to groan.

Kelly grinned, straightened up and began to dust the flour out of her hair. "I had you guys going there, didn't I?"

"Not for a minute," Craig answered. "Say, who swiped my teddy bear?"

"Okay, campers, it's time to turn in."

After a few token grumbles, the group drifted off, leaving Kelly, Rick and Michelle relaxing by the fire.

"So far, so good," said Kelly. "I'd say today's Triathlon was a success."

Rick nodded his agreement. "Even dinner wasn't all that bad."

"We'll have to think of a new menu for next summer's campouts." Michelle made a face. "I'm getting tired of sloppy joes."

"If we're here next year," Kelly said.

"What do you mean?" asked Rick.

"I overheard Mr. Kincaid talking to Bennie the other day. He told him that things are going to be very different at Ash Lake next year."

"I wonder what he meant," Michelle said.

"Who knows?" answered Kelly. "He sure has some funny ideas about running a camp."

"I've noticed," agreed Rick.

Their conversation was interrupted as Craig and Jonathan ran up, breathing hard.

"I thought you said there wasn't anyone else on this island," Craig panted.

"There isn't," Rick assured him.

"But we just saw lights," Jonathan said. "On the far side of the island." He pointed beyond the outhouses. "Over that way."

Rick stood up. "If this is a practical joke . . ."

The boys shook their heads, then led him up the slope to where they had seen the lights flickering a few moments before.

"I can't see anything." Rick surveyed the darkness for any sign of lights. There were only the lengthening shadows of trees.

"They were there a minute ago," Craig insisted.

"Maybe it was a boat on the water," speculated Rick. "Someone might have been shining a flashlight this way."

Jonathan shrugged his shoulders and turned to go back to the campsite.

"Spooks?" a voice queried from the darkness.

Jonathan jumped in his tracks. "Amber Mitchell — how long have you been standing there?"

"Long enough." Amber's braces glinted in the moonlight. "I didn't think you boys would be nervous about staying on the island," she teased.

"We aren't," Craig protested. "We saw lights."

"What's going on?" Liz came up the path behind Amber.

"Craig and Jonathan have been seeing things."

"*Amber!*"

"Whatever you saw," Rick said, "it isn't there now. Ten more minutes," he added as he headed back towards the camp.

"Must have been Weird Walter's pet werewolf again, right?" Liz said.

Craig hunched his shoulders and drew his

hands up like claws. "I'm going to suck zee blood from your neck . . . "

"That's Dracula, you jerk!"

"Oh."

* * *

Liz burrowed deeper into her sleeping bag. Maybe counting sheep would take her mind off it, she thought.

One, two, three . . . No, that wasn't working either. There was no way around it. She had to go.

As quietly as possible, Liz crawled out of her sleeping bag. Amber was lying beside her, sound asleep.

"Amber," Liz whispered and shook her. "Wake up."

"Hmmm?" Amber stirred, but kept on sleeping.

Liz tried again.

"What?" Amber opened her eyes and found Liz centimetres from her face. "What do you want?"

"I've got to go to the bathroom," Liz whispered urgently.

"So?"

"So I'm not going alone!"

Amber plucked the edge of her sleeping bag protectively. "Nooo . . . I'm too comfortable."

"Amber!"

"Oh, all right. What time is it anyway?"

Liz held up her arm and read her watch by the faint light of the moon shining through the tent window. "It's either twenty after three or quarter after four."

Amber groaned. "You owe me for this one, Liz Elliot."

Liz grabbed her flashlight and they tiptoed through the obstacle course of sleeping bodies. Carefully, they unzipped the tent and slipped out into the night.

Eerie shadows crisscrossed the clearing. There wasn't a sound as the two girls glided through the moonlight and into the dark woods.

"Turn on your flashlight, Liz. I can't see a thing."

The light snapped on and bushes leapt out of the darkness. Amber shivered. Liz shone the flashlight on the dirt path in front of them. Every little crack and tree root took on a weird shape, like craters on the moon. The snap of twigs under their feet echoed sharply.

"I don't remember the outhouse being this far from camp," said Liz, anxiously scanning the woods.

"It's over there." Amber pointed off to her left.

Liz swung the light in that direction. Two yellow eyes glowed back at her.

"*Aaaamber!* Let's get out of here!"

"*Oooohhh!*"

They wheeled and ran, pounding through the underbrush until they were out of breath.

"Did you see the size of that animal?" Liz panted.

"It must be a mutant. They don't make raccoons that big," agreed Amber, looking back through the underbrush cautiously.

"Let's forget the facilities," Liz decided. "Stand guard while I duck behind this tree."

A minute later she was back. "Okay, let's get back to the camp."

"Which way?"

Slowly, Liz beamed the flashlight around them. "We walked that way, then ran this way. I'm sure the tents must be over there."

They started back through the woods, warily watching for any sign of wildlife. After a few minutes, the path was still not in sight.

"I thought this was the way we came," Amber said.

"So did I," Liz muttered. "If we get out of this, I swear I'll never have another drink after dinner again."

"Let's try this way," said Amber, taking the flashlight.

"We just came from that way."

"Great, we'll reverse our tracks."

"We have to be logical," Liz chanted as she trudged through the underbrush behind Amber and the bobbing flashlight. "We have to be calm." She shrieked as a branch waved in her face.

"Amber, why are we here? We could be at home. In real beds. With electric lights and flush toilets. Do you realize we could be lost out here forever — two more ghosts on Skull Island."

"Calm and logical, Elliot, remember?"

"I'm trying."

Amber took a few more steps, then slowly swung the light over the trees. The beam flickered eerily from trunk to trunk. She swallowed, took a deep breath, and turned back to Liz.

"Listen, this is an island, right? So no matter which direction we go in, we come to water."

"Unless we walk in circles," Liz pointed out.

Amber began picking her way cautiously along what might have been a path. Reluctantly, Liz followed.

"You know, we could wait here until morning. Like mothers tell their kids — stay put until someone finds you."

"With our luck, you know who it will be — Craig and Jonathan to the rescue. Again."

"You're right. I'd rather meet the ghost."

* * *

The sun was just coming up over the water when Amber and Liz broke out of the woods.

"Campsite ahead," announced Amber.

"Finally," said Liz. "I'll even be glad to see

Jane!" But after another few steps, the two girls stopped dead in their tracks.

"We're not camped this close to the water," Liz said.

"And there's only one tent here . . . "

The single tent stood about thirty metres from the girls in a small clearing very like the one they had started in. But it was different. Wilting branches from uprooted bushes formed a semicircle around the tent on the beach side, hiding the canvas from passing boats. Canned provisions, a jug of water and a cooler were neatly stacked near the front flap, and a small wisp of steam rose from the damp embers of a campfire.

"Weird. The camp owns this island. Nobody else should be here," said Liz.

"I guess someone's trespassing."

"Now what?"

"I believe this is the part where we should beat a strategic retreat," Amber said thoughtfully. "But I sure would like to know whose camp this is."

"Oh, no you don't." Liz pulled Amber's arm firmly. "I've had enough for one night. Let's find *our* camp."

"Just a quick look," Amber insisted as she set off for the tent.

"Hey, wait for me."

They were halfway across the clearing when

the unmistakable whine of a motorboat cut through the morning mist. It was headed for the island.

"What do you think?" Liz asked.

Amber hesitated. The boat's motor revved down as it neared the beach. "Retreat!" she hissed.

The girls did an about-face and raced back into the shelter of the trees. Keeping the shoreline on their left, they ran along the edge of the woods, away from the hidden camp.

6

Who Stole the Cookies
From the Cookie Jar?

The sun was well over the horizon by the time Amber and Liz reached the edge of the camp.

"I'm starving," Liz declared, rubbing her complaining stomach. She sniffed the air. "I smell the campfire, but no sizzling bacon yet."

"Hey, what's going on?" asked Amber. "Look, they're striking the tents."

"But we're supposed to stay until after lunch. Something must be wrong."

The two girls hurried over to a group of campers standing by the remains of the campfire.

"I tell you, it wasn't my fault," Irwin was pleading. "How was I to know the island is infested with wildlife?"

"Irwin," Kelly said with strained calm, "this is nature. These are woods. Animals like raccoons and opossums live in woods. They raid campsites for free meals. Didn't you ever watch *Yogi Bear*?" she shouted.

"What happened?" Amber asked Cathy.

"Irwin got hungry and raided the supplies," Cathy told her. "But he didn't bother to fasten up the packs or containers."

"Oh, no," Liz moaned. "Does that mean breakfast — "

"The coons and possums ate well," Michelle told her. "What they left has to be thrown out."

"I don't believe this camp," Jane declared. "You'd think that someone would have warned Irwin. I mean, it's obvious he doesn't have a lot of self-control."

Irwin stepped closer to Jane until their eyes were scant centimetres apart. "If I had no self-control," he growled, "you would be in the lake right now!"

"Down, Irwin," Rick told him. "C'mon, guys. There's no grub until we get back to the main camp."

"Paddle back on an empty stomach? That's inhuman!" Amber protested.

"Don't be so juvenile," Jane told her. "You could use a diet anyway."

"And you could use a lobotomy." Amber grabbed her knapsack from the pile on the ground and stomped away.

"Don't feel bad," Liz consoled Irwin. "Those raccoons are monsters. We saw one in the woods."

"Thanks," Irwin said. "And everybody, I'm prepared to recompense you all. Look." He unzipped his knapsack.

"I don't think this calls for designer toilet paper," Cathy told him.

"Chocolate bars," he announced. "My whole stock. Only a dollar each."

"Irwin!"

"All right, all right. Free." He sighed and wiped his face. "Never let it be said that I don't make good my mistakes."

"Irwin, even though we hate you," Annette said a minute later as she took a bite of chocolate, "I can honestly say I love you."

"Thank you — I think." Irwin sank down onto a large rock and looked mournfully at the campers happily gulping down his candy.

"Was that your whole stock?" Liz asked.

"Yeah, but these are my friends. I can replace the candy."

"Don't bet on it," Jane smirked.

"What do you mean by that?"

"I mean that the only place to buy candy around here is the general store, which is off limits — unless, of course, you collect the mail for Mr. Kincaid, like I do. I just might use this opportunity to pick up a few things that other people will appreciate."

"Sweetheart, are you trying to muscle in on my racket?"

Jane snickered. "It's called free enterprise, Irwin."

Irwin stood up slowly. "Then, Ms Dobbs, this means war."

* * *

"The lake sure seems wider this morning," Amber said as the canoe slowly approached the camp dock.

"That's because we were up half the night, remember?"

Without the thrill of the Triathlon, or even the comfort of breakfast, the trip back to the main camp had been silent.

"Um," Amber replied. She paused to push her damp hair from her eyes. "Elliot, Liz, isn't that a police car over there?"

Liz squinted into the light. "Sure is. Not another disaster, I hope."

"Come on. Let's find out what's going on."

The girls paddled harder, and soon glided in beside the dock. Amber hopped out to fasten the bow rope, then trotted toward the beach.

"Hey, Amber," Liz called. "What about our packs?"

"Leave them. We've got to find out what the police are doing here." Liz shrugged, climbed out of the canoe and ran after.

A small knot of people had gathered by the tuck shop door, including a middle-aged, slightly rotund man. He was listening intently to Mrs. Dainty.

"Amber, look!" Liz grabbed her arm. "It's Detective Dexter."

Amber grinned. "Maybe Officer Jones is here, too."

Liz groaned. The girls knew both officers from their encounter with the computer pirates at Ash Grove Junior High.

"I don't know how they got in, Detective Dexter," the cook was saying as they reached the group. "Or where they got the key. All I know is that when I opened the cash box for Mr. Kincaid this morning, it was empty."

"She looks ready to cry," Liz whispered.

"Officer," Weird Walter Kincaid said impatiently, "this is really a camp matter. I'd prefer it if you would let me handle the problem."

"Hmm, maybe." Detective Dexter hitched up his pants and looked around at the staff and campers. "How much money was stolen?" he asked abruptly.

"Nearly forty dollars," Mrs. Dainty sniffed.

"As you can see," Weird Walter scoffed, "this is hardly grand theft. I can't imagine why Mr. Sharkman called you."

"Because we're old friends," Jaws answered, appearing from around the corner of the building. "Hello, Louie," he added, shaking hands with the detective.

"Good to see you, Eugene," Dexter said. "Has my boy been learning anything?"

Just then, Irwin, Craig and Jonathan sauntered over to the tuck shop.

"Dad!" Irwin said in surprise. "What are you doing here?"

"Just checking a reported theft, son. I see you've met Craig and Jonathan."

"Yeah. We share a cabin."

"Wonderful! They're the boys who did all that fancy programming at Ash Grove Junior High a while back."

"Yes, they're the best two programmers I have," Jaws added.

"Glad to hear it," Dexter said. "I want Irwin to learn everything he can about computers."

"You bet, Dad." Irwin eyed Craig and Jonathan thoughtfully, then threw an arm around each of their shoulders. "Well, we gotta go. Come on, guys." He dragged Jonathan and Craig off toward the computer room.

"Irwin *Dexter?*" Amber began to giggle. "I

wonder if his dad knows he's into black market candy bars?"

"I'll take a look around for signs of forced entry," Dexter told telling Kincaid. "And Mrs. Dainty, I'd like you to show me the cash box."

"Really, that isn't necessary," Kincaid told him.

"I'll decide that," Dexter replied. "I heard you've had a fire as well," he pulled open the screen door and stepped into the tuck shop.

"Campers," Kincaid spoke loudly, "please return to your activities immediately. Mr. Sharkman, I believe you have a computer session scheduled during this period?"

Jaws nodded curtly and strode off toward the computer room. Most of the campers quietly melted down the paths toward their assigned sessions. Amber and Liz stepped around the corner of the building, out of Weird Walter's view.

Amber's eyes narrowed. "Elliot, I have a very bad feeling about all this."

"Me, too. I wish we knew what was going on in there."

"Let's see if there's an open window at the back," Amber suggested. "That way we can hear everything."

Luckily, all three screened windows at the rear of the building were unshuttered. "Let me climb on your shoulders," Amber whispered.

"Get real. Try those trees." Liz pointed to the

poplars clumped behind the building. As silently as possible, the two girls shinnied and scrambled up the thin trunks. Within the gloom of the shop, they could make out the figures of Kincaid, Detective Dexter and Mrs. Dainty.

"You see, sir," Mrs. Dainty was saying, "I keep the cash box right here under the counter. It's supposed to be locked, but this morning it wasn't. And all the money was gone, too. I just don't understand it."

"Could any of the kids have taken the money?"

"I don't see how," she replied. She peered around the room as if the culprit might be lurking in the shadows. "It would be easy enough to slip the latch on the door, I suppose, but the lock on this box hasn't been broken, and I don't know where one of the campers would get a key."

"Quite a puzzle," Dexter replied. "There doesn't seem to be anything else I can do at the moment, so I'll be heading back to town. Please keep in touch, Mr. Kincaid, if anything else like this occurs. With my boy staying here, I do have a personal interest." He nodded to them both and left the cabin.

"Mrs. Dainty," Kincaid said, leaning close to the cook, "when I hired you, I got the impression that your financial situation was, shall we say, precarious?"

"You might have that impression, Mr. Kincaid," Mrs. Dainty replied sharply, "but I can't see that it's any of your business."

"You're quite right, it *is* none of my business — but this theft is. I didn't call the police because I noticed your reluctance about opening the cash box for me this morning."

"I was in the middle of making breakfast."

"I'm not making any accusations, Mrs. Dainty. I value you as a cook too much for that. But if the forty dollars is somehow returned to the cash box within the next twenty-four hours, I'll be willing to forget it was ever missing."

"*Mr. Kincaid!*"

Kincaid shook his head and left the cabin. From their perch in the trees, Amber and Liz watched Mrs. Dainty pull a handkerchief from her pocket, wipe her nose, then slam shut the lid of the cash box.

"Let's get out of here," Amber whispered. The girls dropped to the ground and dashed for the dock before Mrs. Dainty left the tuck shop.

"That doesn't sound like Mrs. Dainty," Amber spoke thoughtfully as she and Liz began to unload their canoe.

Liz agreed. "I can't imagine why she would swipe money from the tuck shop."

"Maybe she borrowed it," Amber suggested. "You know, planning to put it back on payday. Kincaid said she has money problems."

"Yeah," said Liz as she swung her knapsack

onto the dock. "Maybe we've been wrong about Weird Walter. Maybe he was trying to be nice — letting her put the money back without telling the cops. He sure made it sound slimy though."

* * *

The cafeteria door was latched when Amber and Liz tried it.

"Sorry, girls," Kelly said as she came up the path. "With all the uproar this morning, I couldn't so much as beg some extra muffins."

"But we're in the final throes of terminal starvation!" pleaded Amber.

Kelly laughed. "It's only two hours until lunch. Why not go do crafts for awhile? They're making wallets this morning. See you later." She continued along the path towards the camp offices.

"I'd probably just embarrass us both by chewing up the leather," Liz said. "Say, Amber, what about Irwin? He must have something else stashed away besides toilet paper."

"Sure," Amber agreed. "But we'll need some cash. I think we exhausted Irwin's charity this morning."

Back at the cabin, Jane was sitting cross-legged on her bunk, writing numbers in a small notebook. Brenda, Annette and Cathy were flopped out on their bunks eating doughnuts.

"Food," Liz declared. "Where'd you get those?"

"Jane's selling them," Cathy told her. "Seventy-five cents each. Stale, too. But we were desperate."

"If you weren't cabinmates, it would have been a dollar each," Jane told her.

"Gee, thanks, Jane. What a pal," Brenda murmured.

"I have two plain and a chocolate left," Jane told Amber and Liz. "Fresh, the day before yesterday."

"Forget it," Amber snapped. "We'll go check Irwin."

"We already did," Annette replied. "He was telling us the truth when he said we ate his whole stock this morning."

"That's right," Jane said. "I've cornered the market — and prices are going up. Ninety cents for each doughnut now."

"I'd rather starve to death!" Amber retorted.

"So starve," Jane said sweetly. "I have lots of customers. Oh, and there is a dollar surcharge for special orders when I go pick up the mail this afternoon for Mr. Kincaid."

"Let's get out of here," Amber said. "Ash Lake has spawned a monster."

Liz nodded and they stalked out of the cabin. "As long as Kincaid keeps getting a lot of mail," Liz said, "there's not much we can do about her."

"Oh, yeah?" Amber replied. "I have an idea . . ."

7

Night Raid

"I love it," Irwin whispered. A diabolical smile spread over his wide cheeks.

"I hate it," Craig said, flopping down on the beach beside his friends. He ripped open the small bag of banana chips he had just purchased at the tuck shop.

"Just for the record, I hate it, too," Jonathan added. "But I've got to do something quick. I think I'm starting to like dried apricots. Even when they're covered with sand."

"They taste like grungy Jell-O," Craig replied. "Try one of these." He passed Jonathan a piece of his coin-sized fruit.

Jonathan held it gingerly between his thumb

and index finger. "I refuse to put this in my mouth."

"That's why we need to bring in outside suppliers," Amber insisted. "It's a beautiful plan."

"But, Amber," Liz said through a mouthful of sunflower seeds, "it's a criminal plan."

"That depends on how you look at it."

"We could call Irwin's father for a free consultation." Liz ate the last of her sunflower seeds and scrunched up the bag. "There sure wasn't much to eat today. Even the tuck shop is short of supplies."

Craig shrugged. "We weren't supposed to show up for lunch, and Mrs. Dainty was too upset about the tuck shop money to think about making extra food. I sure hope Kincaid doesn't fire her."

"He can't do that!" Liz protested. "She didn't take the money."

"How do you know?" Jonathan demanded.

"I know," Liz told him. "Gut instincts."

"I get the same ones myself," Irwin agreed, patting his stomach. "Now, if we could get back to the problem at hand? Are we, or are we not, going to use the computers to order a few goodies?"

"Not!" Craig and Jonathan said together.

"Guys!" Amber wailed. "Do you want Jane to rob us all blind?"

Craig pulled a package of gum from his

pocket and smirked. "She's not robbing *all* of us, Amber. I got this at cost."

"I'm surrounded by traitors!"

"Maybe, but we're not starving," Craig replied. "Jonathan, shall we pick up a couple of chocolate bars?"

"I'm with you."

The two boys got up and sauntered over to the picnic table where Jane was besieged by a horde of new friends. Amber and Liz watched in disgust as Jonathan leaned on the table on one side of Jane, and Craig leaned on the other. Craig smiled and began talking.

"They'll be sorry," Amber said. She leaned back on her elbows and idly watched the boats bobbing in the gentle swell. The damaged paddleboat was still overturned on the beach. Bennie was bending over the hull, examining the hole.

"Hey, Liz, Bennie's finally getting around to fixing the boat."

Liz rolled over and looked towards the dock. "As long as we don't get stuck with the bill," she said gloomily.

"All the more reason to go along with Amber's plan," commented Irwin. "A little cash donation to the camp coffers would probably get you off the hook — no pun intended."

The girls groaned. Irwin wiggled his pudgy toes in the sand. Camp, he was discovering, was a thoroughly enjoyable experience.

Over by the picnic table, Craig and Jonathan were looking at Jane with increasing fury. Abruptly, they stomped back to where the others were lounging in the sun.

"Amber," Craig declared, "your plan sounds a lot better all of a sudden. She wants two bucks a chocolate bar!"

Irwin grinned up at him. "Jane doesn't yet understand the basics of good business."

"Shall we say midnight, beside the cafeteria?" Amber smiled sweetly.

"You're on," Jonathan agreed.

Craig glowered in Jane's direction, then nodded.

* * *

"If the girls don't show up soon," Irwin leaned against the cafeteria, "we'd better go on without them. After all, you're the ones who know how to hook up to the wholesalers' computers."

"No way," Jonathan replied grimly. "If we get caught, I want those two there with us."

"Gee, Jonathan," Amber said from the shadowed path, "we didn't think you cared so much."

"Sorry we're late," Liz said breathlessly. "Jane kept counting her money until Michelle threatened to strangle her. Then it was ages before everyone fell asleep and we could sneak out."

"Jane will pay," Craig said. "Did you bring your flashlights?"

"Yes," Amber replied. "Is everything set?"

"Yup," Irwin replied briskly. "I have the phone numbers right here to hook up the modems. And I've worked out a trial supply list based on — "

"Shh!" Jonathan hissed. "Someone might hear us."

"Who?"

"I don't know. Maybe Weird Walter. Or the prowler we ran into before."

"What?" Irwin demanded. "What prowler?"

"Not now," Craig ordered. "Let's get this job over with. I don't even want to think what'll happen if my dad finds out what we're doing."

"*Your* dad!" Irwin replied. "What about my dad?"

"He's got you there," said Amber.

Silently, the five walked along the side of the building and around back, away from the light of the lamppost in the centre of camp. As they passed the back door to the kitchen, Amber, then Irwin, faltered to a stop.

"Hey, guys," Irwin said plaintively, "while we're here . . . It's been hours since dinner."

"I could use a snack," said Craig.

"Sounds good to me," Amber agreed.

Liz and Jonathan looked at each other and shook their heads.

"Great. The majority rules," Amber declared. "Let me just deal with this door here."

Efficiently, she pulled out her pocketknife, opened the blade, and used it to slide the latch.

"B & E," Jonathan commented. "My mother was really excited about all the things I'd learn at camp."

"This is entering," Amber corrected him. "There is no breaking involved."

"Besides, it's for a great cause," Irwin added.

Quietly, the five of them went into the darkened kitchen. "This way," Amber said, moving confidently towards the big refrigerators at the back. "No lights. We don't want anyone to see us."

"Why is it that we spend so much time at this camp creeping around in the dark or scrounging for food?" Liz leaned against the counter with her arms folded while Amber, Irwin and Craig rummaged in the fridge.

"It's because you and Amber keep sticking your noses in where they don't belong," Jonathan retorted.

"Cheesecake," Craig said from inside the fridge, his voice muffled. "Definitely cheesecake." He pulled out a large cake, loosely wrapped in plastic.

"Fabulous!" Irwin declared, licking his lips. "And there's a couple of pieces missing already, so who'll ever know?"

"Here's a knife," Amber announced, brandishing a large kitchen knife. "Let's divide it — "

"Quiet!" Jonathan hissed suddenly. They froze. There was the unmistakable sound of footsteps in the dining hall.

"Oh, no," Liz moaned softly. "Not again!"

"Hide!" Jonathan commanded.

Amber and Liz dove under the same table as before. A second later, Irwin, Craig and Jonathan crowded in with them.

"Find your own table," Amber whispered furiously.

"Shut up, Amber."

The footsteps moved across the wooden floor. Two large shadows loomed along the wall. Cautiously, Amber peered out. It was Mrs. Dainty and a stranger. The man paused near the door and watched the cook. The kids held their breath.

Liz's eyes focussed on the cheesecake, still sitting on the counter. "Oh, no," she whispered, pointing at the cake. "We're dead."

Quiet! Craig mouthed.

They hardly dared to breathe as Mrs. Dainty opened one of the far cupboards, rummaged way at the back, then finally pulled out a coffee can.

"What's this?" she said suddenly, dropping the coffee can with a loud bang on the metal counter. The kids cowered down as she stalked towards the cheesecake.

"Please don't turn around," Amber breathed.

Mrs. Dainty stood staring for a moment, hands on her hips, back to the kids. Then she scooped up the cake, wrapper and knife. Deftly she rewrapped the cake, put it away in the fridge, and dropped the knife into the metal sink. It clanged eerily in the silent kitchen.

Liz tugged at Amber's shirt-tail and silently pointed towards the man in the shadows. Who is he? she mouthed. Amber shrugged and put her finger to her lips.

"I wish I'd never taken this job. The things I do for you . . ." Mrs. Dainty spoke angrily. "Even if you find out what you want to, what good will it do you?"

Amber and Liz glanced at each other. Mrs. Dainty picked up the coffee can again, pulled off the lid, and took out a handful of crumpled bills. Quickly, she counted some out and handed them to the stranger.

"That's all. And don't come looking for any more either. I'm in so much trouble now, you'd better lie low until things settle down."

"Thanks," he said quietly. "I won't need any more money — for a while anyway. Are you sure you can handle it, Rose?"

"I've handled the likes of Kincaid before," said Mrs. Dainty. "Now, go on. Get out of here before someone sees you."

The man slipped out the screen door into the night.

"Honestly, why I do this . . . " Mrs. Dainty grumbled to herself. A moment later she went into the dining hall. The kids could hear her feet on the wooden floor, then the unmistakable *creak, bang,* and *click* as she went out the front door and locked it behind her.

"Whew," Irwin breathed. Awkwardly, they all crawled out from under the table.

"That must have been the tuck shop money!" Craig exclaimed. "I never would have believed Mrs. Dainty could be a crook."

"And who was the guy?" Jonathan demanded. "Anyone ever seen him around before? He could be her accomplice."

"You two are jumping to conclusions," Amber declared. "Mrs. Dainty can't be a thief. She's too good a cook."

"Amber," Craig said patiently, "you've got to look at the facts. We saw her."

"Saw her what? Give some of her own hard-earned cash to a . . . a . . . friend?"

"What friend?" Craig demanded. "That guy shouldn't be here. This is private property. And it's the middle of the night! There's something very fishy about Mrs. Dainty and this whole set-up."

"I think you're wrong, Craig," Liz interrupted. "Mrs. Dainty's not the type."

"I agree," Irwin interjected.

"But whether or not Mrs. Dainty is the tuck

shop thief, it's obvious she's doing something she shouldn't."

"No way!" Amber retorted. "Mrs. Dainty is innocent, and we're going to prove it."

"How?" Jonathan asked. When Amber didn't answer, he shrugged and shook his head. "Sleep on it, Amber."

"Right," agreed Craig, yawning widely. "I'm for bed."

"Bed?" Amber demanded. "How can you go to bed now? Do you think the Hardy Boys went to bed in the middle of a case?"

"The Case of the Mysterious Prowler," Liz interjected.

"Don't forget, we still have work to do," Irwin reminded them. "Nothing will be better tomorrow if we don't do something about it tonight."

Silence, then Craig heaved a sigh. "All right. But if we get caught, Amber Mitchell, I'm telling them that you're responsible for everything."

Amber nodded curtly. "Let's go." Silently, they filed out the kitchen door and into the night.

"Think the prowler might still be around?" Liz asked nervously as they crept along the path.

"Probably not," Jonathan whispered back. "He'll be getting out of here as quick as he can." A moment later they heard the coughing roar of a motorboat starting up.

"You're right," Liz agreed with relief. "He's on his way back to the island."

"The island?" Jonathan demanded, stopping dead. Irwin crashed into him, nearly knocking him over.

"*Oof!*"

"Watch it!"

"Quiet!" Amber hissed. "You'll wake someone up. We'll tell you about it later." Jonathan and Craig looked at her in disbelief, but she ignored them and crept on.

It was pitch dark by the door to the computer building.

"This is strange," Craig muttered. "Look, the door's unlocked. I didn't think Jaws would ever be that careless."

"So, we'll lock up afterwards and cover for him," Irwin replied. "Let's go."

As they went into the building, Liz hesitated and looked in either direction across the dark campground. "I've got a bad feeling," she said quietly.

"Relax," Amber told her. "You'll feel a lot better when the cupcakes start to arrive."

"Quick," Irwin called briskly. "A strike force hasn't got time to stand around."

"Strike force?"

"Jonathan, Craig, man those computers. Amber and Liz, you hold the flashlights. We can't risk turning on the lights."

"Yes, *mon capitaine,*" Craig saluted.

Irwin didn't notice. Caught in the excitement

of his coup, he stood in the centre of the room, surveying the preparations and studying his list.

"All right, Craig, you'll make contact with Green Garden Wholesalers, Inc. Here's your information." He thrust a piece of paper into Craig's hand.

Amber shone the flashlight on the paper for a moment, then shrugged. As far as she could see, it was just a list with some numbers on it.

Craig, however, seemed to know what to do. While Irwin gave a second list to Jonathan, Craig turned on his computer and selected a modem. A few seconds later he began typing in commands. At the next table, Jonathan followed the same steps, but with a different wholesaler.

"We want comparative prices," Irwin ordered.

"Irwin," Jonathan protested, "we don't have time to shop around!"

"That's a terrible way to run a business," Irwin retorted.

"Who's paying for all this?" Liz asked.

"We are. As long as you have an account at these places, you have thirty days to pay," Irwin told her.

"But we don't have an account."

"The camp does. I borrowed an old invoice from Kincaid's office this afternoon. Does he ever get a lot of mail! I nearly got caught going through his desk. We'll bill the camp, but send the deliveries care of I. Dexter, Dexter Enterprises. That way, we can realize our profits and pay the bill before . . . "

". . . before your father comes to arrest us," Jonathan finished. "Dexter Enterprises." He shook his head. "How'd we ever get into this anyway?"

"Jane," Amber answered.

"And Weird Walter," Liz added.

"Quit worrying. It's all for a good cause," Irwin reminded them with hearty enthusiasm. "Make sure you key in that this is all a rush order — immediate delivery."

"Liz, hold that flashlight still," Craig commanded suddenly.

"I thought I heard something."

"You're just getting spooked," Craig replied. "There, I'm done. This better work, Irwin, old buddy, because I just ordered a hundred and twelve dollars worth of junk food."

"All right!"

"Ninety-eight worth here," Jonathan reported as he switched off his machine and replaced the modem. "Now, let's make sure everything is left exactly the way it was when we got here. I don't want to be connected with any part of this scam."

Carefully, they looked around and straightened anything that might have been knocked ajar.

"Okay, you guys go out first," Craig ordered. "I'll make sure this door is locked behind us. That prowler could come back, and who knows what he's up to."

Silently, the five campers slipped out the door. The only sound in the night was the firm click as the door locked behind them.

8

Something's Fishy at Ash Lake

The sun was well up over the trees before Liz opened her eyes. Blearily, she looked around the cabin. Empty — even Amber's bunk.

Liz stared out the screen window by her bed until the cabin door slammed several minutes later.

"It's about time you woke up," Amber said. She sat down on the end of Liz's bunk, dropping a paper bag beside her. "Michelle thought something was wrong with you — she kept shaking you and you kept mumbling and going back to sleep. You missed breakfast by an hour.

We've got computers in ten minutes."

Liz yawned. "I think I'll stay here until lunch."

"Not a chance." Amber grabbed Liz by the arm and pulled her into a sitting position. "We have a crime to solve."

Liz rubbed her eyes. "I was hoping I'd dreamed it all."

Amber shook her head. "It happened all right. But so far, just you, me, Jonathan, Craig and Irwin know about Mrs. Dainty's prowler. He left in a motorboat, so he's got to be the person camping on Skull Island. If Kincaid finds out about that meeting last night . . . "

" . . . he'll fire Mrs. Dainty for sure," finished Liz. "But if that was the tuck shop money she gave the prowler, why would she risk her job for a lousy forty bucks?"

"That's what we have to find out."

"Now?"

"Now."

"But Amber, I haven't even had breakfast yet. I can't possibly investigate on an empty stomach." Liz lay back down.

"That's why I brought you some muffins." Amber tossed the paper bag at Liz with a grin. "Now eat, get dressed, and let's get on with this case."

Liz reached inside the bag. "Mmm, wild blueberry muffins." She took a bite. "Amber," she said, "we *have* to clear Mrs. Dainty. These are fabulous."

"If we're going to clear Mrs. Dainty, we have to figure out who that prowler is and why she's giving him money."

"Maybe he's blackmailing her," Liz suggested, her mouth full of muffin.

"That's not a bad idea," agreed Amber. She jumped to her feet and began pacing the floor of the cabin. "Maybe she's had a shady past and somebody's threatening to tell Weird Walter." She stopped and narrowed her eyes in speculation. "I'll bet it has something to do with that tattoo."

Liz licked her fingers. "Amber, if you ask me, you've had a little too much sun. He's probably just a friend that she's lending money to."

"In the middle of the night?" Amber demanded. "That doesn't make sense."

"Does anything around here?" Liz hesitated. "I've been thinking about that fire in the generator. What if it wasn't an accident after all?"

"We can check that out, too," Amber told her. "But we've only got one more week to figure out everything, so get up!" She rummaged around in Liz's duffle bag. "Here," she added, throwing a T-shirt and shorts in Liz's direction. "Only Batman and Robin solve crimes in their underwear."

* * *

Mrs. Dainty was seated at one of the tables, lists spread around her, when Liz and Amber cautiously peeked into the dining hall. They looked carefully in the direction of Kincaid's office, but there was no light behind the frosted glass of the door.

"Remember, subtlety," Liz whispered.

They hurried over to the table and slid into seats opposite the cook.

"Hi!" Amber began brightly.

Mrs. Dainty looked up and smiled. "Good morning. You girls are early for kitchen detail."

"Oh, we're not here to help," Amber denied hastily.

"What she means," Liz interrupted, "is that it isn't our turn at lunch today. We, uh, dropped by on our way to computers to tell you how great those muffins were this morning."

"That's right," Amber agreed. She paused. "I'll bet Mr. Dainty sure misses your cooking."

"Hmph," Mrs. Dainty replied. "Does it look like I have a Mr. Dainty to cook for? Drat these menus! Mr. Kincaid keeps changing them so that I have to reorder supplies. It makes my budget come out all wrong."

"You mean Mr. Dainty is . . . is . . . " Liz faltered.

"That's right," Mrs. Dainty said grimly. "And I'm here coping with Mr. Kincaid." She sighed. "That man could try a saint."

"That's for sure," Amber agreed.

"I guess doing all the ordering is really difficult," Liz said sympathetically.

"Oh, not if you know how," Mrs. Dainty replied as she added two more items to the list she was making. "When we owned the marina, I did all the orders for the grocery and snack bar."

"You did?"

"Yes, before — " Mrs. Dainty stopped, then glanced uncertainly at the girls. "Enough of this," she said instead. "I have work to do, and I can't waste my time chattering." She stood up abruptly, gathered her lists, and disappeared into the kitchen.

"She must be a widow," Liz said.

Amber nodded wisely. "I guess she's too choked up to talk about it."

* * *

Amber and Liz skidded to a stop on the path leading to the computer building. Campers were swarming around the open door. A police car was pulled up to one side of the building. A uniformed officer was taking notes as Walter Kincaid paced in front of the door, shouting angrily.

"This has gone too far! What am I going to tell the Board of Directors? Sharkman, where are you?"

"Oh, boy," Amber said. "I think we both should have stayed in bed until lunch."

Liz opened her mouth, then shut it again. The two girls watched silently as Detective Dexter, accompanied by Mr. Sharkman, came out of the building. Kincaid faced them, his voice lowered but his red face and angry gestures demonstrating his mood.

"It can't be anything we did last night, can it?" Liz asked nervously.

Amber bit her lip. "It can't be. But," she added, "I think we'd better go investigate." Carefully keeping out of Kincaid's line of vision, the girls walked over to the crowd of campers.

"Look, there are the boys," Liz pointed. Irwin, Jonathan and Craig were loitering beside the police car.

"They're keeping a low profile," Amber commented. "Let's get a peek in the door."

As inconspicuously as possible, they sidled past the other campers, stepped onto the porch, and slipped through the open door. Amber's jaw dropped. "This is unbelievable!"

The file cabinets had been tipped over, and all their contents strewn in every direction. Disks with the labels torn off lay scattered amid papers and books. The electric cords for the computers had been tied into knots and tangled around desk legs and chairs. One computer monitor had been knocked to the floor. Broken glass from the screen lay sprayed around it.

"Quite a mess, isn't it?"

Neither Amber nor Liz had heard Jane Dobbs enter the computer lab behind them. Since the doughnut episode, she and Amber had avoided each other whenever possible.

"I'll bet Jaws would love to get his hands on whoever did this. Not to mention Mr. Kincaid," Jane went on. She pushed at some of the broken glass with her sneaker.

Amber turned and glared at the other girl. "Did you want something, Jane? Or are you just passing time?"

"Oh, just passing time," Jane purred. "And trying to decide whether or not to tell Mr. Sharkman about the two empty bunks in Cabin Three last night." She raised her hand and casually examined her fingernails.

Amber took an angry step toward her. "We had nothing to do with this!" She stopped about a nose away from the other girl's face. "And you'll keep your big mouth shut, Jane Dobbs, if you know what's good for you."

Jane stood her ground. "Oh, yeah?" she countered. "Don't you try to threaten me, Amber Mitchell. I could get both you and Liz kicked out of this camp easily if I wanted to." Then she turned on her heel and flounced out.

"One of these days," Amber growled through clenched braces.

Liz shook her head. "Couldn't the two of you call a truce?"

Amber spun around and stared at Liz in disbelief. "If you think I'm going to get buddy-buddy with Jane after what she just said, you're nuts!"

"I don't care if you're friends," declared Liz hotly. "I'm just sick of you two being enemies."

"Never mind," fumed Amber. She looked around the devastated computer lab. "We'd better call an executive meeting of Dexter Enterprises about this."

* * *

"What took you so long?" Craig demanded as Liz and Amber hauled themselves out of the water and onto the wooden diving raft. After their morning computer class had been cancelled, the campers had been rescheduled for swimming.

"We stayed behind to help Jaws clean up," explained Liz.

"And to see if he suspects anyone," Amber added moodily.

"Does he?" Jonathan asked.

"I don't know. He just stared at the mess for a couple of minutes, then muttered, 'How strange . . . this is not right.' That was it." She eyed Irwin's huge yellow and red striped bathing trunks. "What are you wearing? Designer swimwear?"

"Naturally."

"How bad was the damage?" interrupted Craig.

"Not as bad as it looked," Liz reassured him. "Only one monitor is broken. The rest of the stuff was just mixed up."

"Jaws was loading all the disks when we left," added Amber, "trying to match their directories with the labels."

"He didn't say anything?" asked Jonathan.

"Nope." Amber rolled over on her stomach. "He was just muttering something about computers being a mixed blessing. New inventions breed new crimes — that sort of thing."

Irwin swatted at a fly buzzing around his face. "We'd better not try to sell him any of our candy shipment."

"No kidding," agreed Liz. "If he ever finds out we were in the computer room last night . . . "

" . . . we'll be history," concluded Jonathan.

"But if Kincaid doesn't find out who did it, this whole camp could be history anyway," said Craig. "ET won't spend any money to replace the broken equipment. My dad won't look too good either. He really supports the camp." Craig stared out across the lake at Skull Island.

"Do you think this has anything to do with the fire in the generator?" Liz asked finally. She thoughtfully twirled a strand of nearly-dry hair around her finger thoughtfully. "Or Mrs. Dainty's mysterious stranger?"

"It couldn't be him," said Amber. "We heard him leave in the motorboat before we ordered the candy."

"Then who totalled the computer room?" Craig demanded.

"Mrs. Dainty?" Jonathan suggested lamely.

"Get serious!" Amber pulled at her damp bathing suit.

"You're making this unnecessarily complicated," said Irwin. "It was probably just one of the campers."

"Then why wasn't the computer room lock picked?" asked Liz. "Not to mention the tuck shop cash box."

"Humph," Amber grunted. "If Jane Dobbs has her way, Jaws'll think Liz and I are the culprits."

"What?"

"She noticed we weren't in our bunks last night and threatened to tell him," Amber reported bitterly.

"There goes my last guilt pang about the junk food we ordered," said Craig. He glanced at the beach where Jane was lounging on the sand with Annette and Brenda. "At least we'll put her out of business."

"Actually, I rather admire her," Irwin said.

The others stared at him incredulously. "What!"

"Irwin, how could you?"

"She's the goody-two-shoes of Ash Grove!" Craig said.

"She is always sticking her nose in where it doesn't belong and stirring up trouble," conceded Jonathan.

"Just whose side are you on anyway, Irwin Dexter?" demanded Amber.

"It's not a question of sides. But don't you think she'd make a better friend than an enemy?"

Liz watched Amber out of the corner of her eye.

"Never!" Amber got to her feet and dove off the raft into the cool water.

"Well, we know where Amber stands on that one," observed Jonathan. He got up, too, and made a clean dive just as Amber broke the surface of the water a few metres away.

Liz eyed Irwin. "You've got a plan, don't you?"

He nodded. "Let's just say I see a useful part for Jane to play in our future."

"What's that?" asked Craig.

"She's got two things that we don't have," mused Irwin. "Access to the general store, and a job as Kincaid's personal mailman."

"Mailperson," Liz said automatically.

"Whatever."

"So?"

"So," Irwin turned to watch Amber and Jonathan as they swam to the buoys and back, "there are still one or two roadblocks in the way of Dexter Enterprises' rise to fame and fortune."

Craig buried his face in his arms. "I knew it."

"What roadblocks?" demanded Liz.

Irwin cleared his throat. "Just a few minor details."

"Like what?"

"Like convincing Jane to mail our money in to the suppliers."

Craig rolled his eyes. "Good luck!"

"And?" prompted Liz.

"And hijacking the delivery truck before it gets to camp tomorrow."

9

Big Business

Peace had at last settled over the dining hall. The campers had devoured stacks of pancakes and mountains of fresh scrambled eggs, and gone on to their morning activities. Eugene Sharkman was savouring the quiet interlude over a copy of the *Ash Grove Examiner*.

"*Lakefront property getting scarce,*" he read. "This looks interesting." He folded his newspaper back and scanned the article more closely. "*As more and more people head for cottage country, the competition for a stretch of sand is fierce . . .*"

"Coffee, Mr. Sharkman?" Mrs. Dainty stood at his elbow with a steaming coffee pot.

"Yes, please." He put down his newspaper. "Why don't you join me for a cup? It smells delicious."

Mrs. Dainty hesitated, and glanced uneasily around the dining room. Other than Kelly Slemko meeting with her counsellors at a table in the corner, Mr. Sharkman appeared to be the only one around.

"If it's Mr. Kincaid you're looking for," the computer teacher said wryly, "he just went into his office. He said he had several telephone calls to make."

Mrs. Dainty sighed. "In that case, I don't mind if I do. I'll just go and get myself a cup."

"Kincaid is an extremely aggressive administrator," Mr. Sharkman observed when Mrs. Dainty returned. "But I'm not sure he always has the campers' best interests at heart."

She nodded and sat down. "Or the camp's. Besides, I feel like he's looking over my shoulder all the time, just waiting for me to make a mistake."

Mr. Sharkman reached for the sugar bowl. "Cream and sugar?"

"No, thanks."

"Yes, it's as though he wants us to have problems," mused Jaws as he stirred two heaping spoonfuls of sugar into his coffee.

"What do you mean?"

"I can't quite put my finger on it," he said.

"But if Kincaid recommends that Eastern Technology close this camp, scapegoats may be necessary. You and I seem to be the most likely candidates."

"But we haven't done anything!" protested Mrs. Dainty.

"I know," said Mr. Sharkman. "But think how it will look. You're in charge of the tuck shop, and I'm in charge of the computer room. And where have all the problems been?"

"The computer room and the tuck shop," answered Mrs. Dainty.

"Precisely."

The cook took a sip of her coffee. "But what can we do?" she asked. "People like him hold all the cards."

"Let me think about it for a bit," said Mr. Sharkman. "Perhaps I'll call ET's vice-president, Robert Nicholson, myself." He picked up his cup. "They have an expression for it in the business world. It's called covering your, um, your . . . " he faltered.

"Backside," suggested Mrs. Dainty innocently.

Mr. Sharkman blushed. "Right."

"Drink your coffee," Mrs. Dainty told him. "It's getting cold."

The computer teacher raised his cup and took a large gulp. "Yaargh!" He spit it right back.

"Oh, no," cried Mrs. Dainty. "What's wrong?"

Mr. Sharkman's face appeared to shrivel up. "That's not sugar," he gasped, pointing at the bowl. "It's salt!"

"Those kids must be at it again." Mrs. Dainty pressed a hand over her mouth to hide her amusement. "I'll get you a fresh cup." She hurried off towards the kitchen.

Jaws glared at the sugar bowl and cautiously tasted a few grains from the tip of his finger. "Drat this camp! I should have taken that Mediterranean cruise with Miss Belcher," he muttered.

Mrs. Dainty returned a moment later with Liz and Amber in tow. "I put sugar in this myself," she said as she placed another cup of coffee on the table in front of Mr. Sharkman.

Jaws frowned at the girls.

"We're innocent," Amber hastily assured him.

"Honest," added Liz. "We've just been helping in the kitchen."

"Besides," added Amber, "that's an amateur's work. Nobody falls for that old joke. I mean . . . "

Liz jabbed her with her elbow. "Good one, Amber."

"Never mind," said Mr. Sharkman. He took a sip of coffee. "Aaah, that's better."

Mrs. Dainty smiled. "Okay, girls, this is what I want you to do." She picked up the sugar bowl and emptied it into the bucket Liz was holding, then took the sugar canister from Amber and refilled the bowl. "Start at the next table and work your way around the room," she instructed, handing the canister back to Amber.

The girls moved away.

"Poor Mr. Sharkman," giggled Amber under her breath. "He's never going to forget this summer."

"Neither are we," whispered Liz. "Look who's coming," she added a moment later. "Slow down."

Walter Kincaid entered the dining room and strode over to where Mr. Sharkman and Mrs. Dainty were sitting.

"There you are," he grumbled at the cook as though she'd been eluding him all morning. "I just had a call from the delivery man. He'll be delivering our supplies from the wholesalers this afternoon at about one-thirty. Please be available then to check the orders."

Amber nudged Liz. "Bingo!" she whispered. "Now we know what time."

"One of the wholesalers also called," continued Mr. Kincaid. "He seemed a little confused about the order, but he's sending it anyway. You haven't deviated from the approved menu plan, have you?" he asked suspiciously.

Mrs. Dainty shook her head. "Of course not."

"Oh, oh," whispered Liz. "She's going to be in more trouble because of us."

"Don't panic," said Amber. She dumped out another bowlful of salt. "I have a feeling Irwin will come up with something."

* * *

"Toilet paper?"

"The bottom's fallen out of the market," said Irwin, tossing his duffle bag to the ground.

"You're going to stop a truck with toilet paper?" Liz demanded.

"Have you got a better idea?" Irwin wiped his forehead and sat down on the grass beside the girls.

"Rope," suggested Liz.

Irwin shook his head. "The only rope I could find was attached to the boats. Couldn't risk it."

"Where are Craig and Jonathan?" Amber asked. She and Liz searched the dusty road for signs of the boys.

"They'd better hurry up," added Liz. "It's after one o'clock already."

"They're not coming," said Irwin.

"*What?*"

"Rick decided we all had to practise the front crawl before our swimming test on Friday."

"So why aren't you crawling?" Amber asked. Idly she chewed the stem of a long piece of grass.

"I told Rick I had a stomachache."

"And he fell for that?" Liz was amazed.

Irwin patted his stomach. "Rick never argues

over matters concerning my constitution. Besides, he'd have to save me."

"You're incredible." Amber spit out her stalk of grass.

"Yes, I am," Irwin smiled.

Amber stood up and brushed off the seat of her shorts. "Well, let's get started."

"Are you sure this will work, Irwin?"

"Ladies, this is high quality merchandise — we're talking two ply." He unzipped his duffle bag and pulled out a package of toilet paper with a flourish.

"Save the sales pitch, Irwin," Amber said. "Is there enough to go across the road?"

Irwin scrutinized the plastic wrapping. "According to the package, there are 224 sheets on each roll. Each sheet is 15 centimetres long." Irwin frowned in concentration. "That's 3,360 centimetres per roll, which makes . . . 134.4 metres per package."

The girls stared at him. "How did you do that so fast?" Liz demanded.

"When it involves money, I'm a human calculator."

"You're going to be a human sacrifice if we don't hurry up," warned Amber. She grabbed the package of toilet paper and unwrapped it, tossing two rolls to Liz and keeping the rest for herself.

"Hey," protested Irwin, "one roll will do!"

"Better safe than sorry."

"You hold the ends," Amber directed, "while Liz and I unroll the paper."

Irwin frowned, then lumbered into position at the side of the road, muttering under his breath.

"What did he say?" asked Liz.

Amber shrugged. "Something about profit margins, I think."

Five minutes later, Irwin stood in the middle of the road, arms open wide, admiring their work. "Magnificent! A rhapsody in pink."

Amber giggled. "I wish Craig and Jonathan were here to see this."

Liz nodded. "Irwin has flair. Even we would never have thought of T.P.ing the road." Strands of toilet paper crisscrossed the road like tired party streamers.

"All we need are a couple of pink flamingos," Amber said.

"Ssh!" Liz looked down the road. "I think I hear something."

The steady drone of an approaching vehicle cut through the stillness of the woods, growing louder and louder as it approached the camp.

"Quick, off the road!"

The three campers dove into the bushes. A moment later, the delivery truck rounded a curve and screeched to a stop, just centimetres from the fluttering pink barrier.

"What the — " The driver swung down from

the cab of his truck to get a closer look. "Toilet paper? No one will believe this one!"

Irwin parted the bushes and strode out to meet him.

"Sorry for the inconvenience, sir," he said, holding out his hand. "Irwin Dexter, Dexter Enterprises. I believe you have a special shipment for me."

The bewildered driver shook Irwin's hand. "Is this some kind of joke?"

Irwin eyed the man's shirt, embroidered over the pocket with the name *Fred*. Liz and Amber stepped out of the bushes and came to stand beside him. Amber smiled widely, so the sun glinted on her braces.

"No, it's not a joke, Mr. . . . uh . . . Fred," said Irwin. "My partners and I have an order on your truck."

"From Green Garden Wholesalers, Inc.," Amber told him.

"And the Food Factory," added Liz.

Fred looked them over suspiciously. "I picked up some orders from those places," he agreed, "but everything's going to Eastern Technology's computer camp."

"That's right," said Irwin. "Everything except the ones marked *Dexter Enterprises*."

"Just a minute while I check my list." Fred reached inside the cab for his clipboard full of invoices, then flipped through the bills.

"Seems you're right. I. Dexter, Dexter Enterprises."

"That's me."

Fred looked at him.

"Do I need to show you my birth certificate?" Irwin asked anxiously.

"It says here that it's to be delivered care of the camp."

Irwin cleared his throat and glanced at the girls. "Okay, here's the situation." He proceeded to fill the delivery man in on their caper. All three campers watched anxiously as Fred's stern face twitched. Finally, he began to laugh.

"All right, then, Irwin Dexter. If you're sure you can — and will — cover the cost of these famine rations for your camp buddies . . . "

"Yes, sir. Absolutely, sir," Irwin reassured him.

"I'm in the wrong racket," chuckled Fred. "Come on, kids, let's get your order out of the back."

Five minutes later, everything was unloaded and the roadblock was dismantled.

"Give me a call when you hit the big time, Irwin," called Fred as he climbed into his cab. He gave them the thumbs up sign, then the truck rumbled the last half kilometre into camp.

"We did it!" Amber shouted.

"Was there ever any doubt?" Irwin said triumphantly.

"We're not out of the woods yet," cautioned Liz. She picked up one of the boxes. "We've still got to stash this stuff somewhere out of sight."

"Look out, Jane, here we come!" crowed Amber as she grabbed another box.

"Uh, Amber," began Irwin tentatively, "I've been meaning to tell you. It's about Jane . . . "

* * *

"Twenty percent."

"Get serious." Irwin picked up a pebble and tossed it into the calm lake, rippling the reflection of the setting sun. He watched until the water was still again. This was going to be tougher than he thought. "Ten percent," he countered.

Jane doodled in the sand with a twig. "You want me to take your money to the store, buy money orders, and mail them to the wholesalers. For a lousy ten percent!" She slapped at a mosquito. "You're off your nerd."

Irwin flushed. "Now, look, Jane. You go to the store and the post office for Kincaid anyway. It's no big deal."

"Except to you."

"Listen to me. If we don't send the money in before the wholesalers bill the camp, Kincaid will blame Mrs. Dainty."

"So? Why should you care? She stole the tuck shop money, didn't she?"

"Nobody's proved that."

Jane snorted. "It's obvious who you've been hanging out with."

"Oh, nasty."

"So, what's Amber's cut in this deal?" she asked.

"The same as everyone else's," Irwin said cautiously. "We're splitting the profits five ways."

"Make that six and you've got a deal."

Irwin thought about it. "On one condition," he agreed at last, taking a deep breath.

"What condition?"

"You go to the movies with me next month," he blurted out. "My treat."

10

Revenge is . . . Sour

Liz kicked at the lump above her in the top bunk. "Are you going to sulk all day, Amber, or what?"

There was no answer.

"I know you're mad about Jane," continued Liz, "but you don't have to ruin the rest of our vacation."

Still no answer.

Liz sat up and reached for her sneakers. "I don't want to split the profits with Jane either, but if it means keeping Mrs. Dainty out of trouble, then I'm all for it." She finished lacing her shoes and stood up.

Amber lay on her back, staring at the ceiling.

"Do you realize there are four different species of spiders living in here with us?" she said.

"Why do you think I grabbed the bottom bunk?"

Amber suddenly rolled over and swung down from the bed. "I'm only doing this for Mrs. Dainty."

Liz eyed her skeptically.

"Okay, okay, so I want my share of the profits too."

They banged out of their cabin and cut down the path to Cabin Seven. Jonathan, Craig and Irwin were sitting in the grass, waiting. When he saw the girls, Irwin jumped to his feet.

"Hasn't Jane come back from the store yet?" he demanded.

Liz shook her head. "We just came from our cabin. I thought she'd be here."

Craig and Jonathan stood up and joined the others on the path. "She's probably made off with all the profits," Craig said. "Call out your dad, Irwin."

"The sooner, the better," Amber agreed.

"Knock it off, you guys," Irwin told them. "We made a deal," he added with a self-conscious smile. "She'll be here."

"Or else," Amber said.

Jonathan pointed in the direction of the girls' cabin. "Here she comes now."

Irwin dusted off the seat of his pants and

patted his hair in place as Jane came marching up the path, toting a canvas bag full of newspapers and mail.

"What took you so long?" demanded Craig.

"Any problems?" asked Irwin.

Jane caught her breath before she explained. "That witch in the store was mad about all the change. She made me wait until she'd helped everyone else first. And there was a whole bunch of mail."

"Let's just get on with it," Amber said.

"Not here." Craig looked warily towards the main buildings. "The way our luck has been going, Weird Walter will come sauntering up the path."

"Follow me," said Irwin. He led the others to a clearing about fifteen metres behind the cabin. Thick pines cut off the view from the main camp, and several fallen logs provided seating for the board meeting of Dexter Enterprises.

Jane dug into the bag and pulled out a paper sack full of small bills and coins. "Here's what's left over from the money orders and postage." She passed it over to Irwin.

Deftly he emptied out the money, counted it, and divided it into six piles in front of him. Five pairs of eyes watched every move, making sure he didn't short-change anyone.

"Not bad for a night's work," remarked Jonathan as he slipped his share into his pocket.

"Too bad we don't have time to do it again before we go home," Amber agreed.

"Just wait until next year," Irwin said. "Now that we've got the routine down, and with a whole year to work out the details, we'll really clean up."

"Don't count on it," Craig cautioned. "I had a letter from my parents yesterday. Dad says that the Board is serious about pulling out. The way things are going, this place'll probably be closed and sold by next year."

"Not if we can solve this case," Amber declared.

"There are only four days of camp left," Jonathan reminded her. "And so far you haven't made any progress at all."

"We will," Amber told him. "Even if it takes the rest of the summer."

"School starts again in three and a half weeks," Liz said.

Everybody groaned.

"That reminds me," said Jane. She rooted through her bag. "Jaws got a postcard," she held up a picture postcard from Greece, "from Miss Belcher!"

Everyone hooted except Irwin.

"Who's Miss Belcher?" he demanded.

"Our Language Arts teacher," explained Amber. "She's got the hots for Jaws."

"*Dear Eugene*," Jane read, pleased at being

the centre of attention. *"Having a great time. Wish you were here."*

"Original," Liz commented.

"Hope the children are behaving for you. See you in September. With warm regards, Miss B."

"Oooh, Eugene . . . "

Jane snorted and returned the postcard to her bag. "I'd better get this stuff to Kincaid before he gets suspicious."

"Thanks for helping us out, Jane," Irwin said.

Craig and Jonathan added their appreciation. Liz jabbed Amber in the ribs.

"Yeah, Jane, thanks," she said reluctantly. "Now Mrs. Dainty won't get into any more trouble."

"Or us," Liz added.

Jane fixed her gaze at a spot over Amber's head. "I'm sorry about what I said the other day."

"You are?"

Jane cleared her throat. "I wouldn't have told Jaws."

Amber stared at her, then finally nodded. "I accept your apology. And I'm sorry I threatened you."

Irwin shone like a benevolent uncle, while Craig and Jonathan looked from one girl to the other in fascination.

"I don't believe it," said Jonathan.

"If this keeps up, I'm going to puke," Craig added, standing up to go. "Hey, what's this?" He bent over to pick up an envelope that had fallen half under the log.

"It's addressed to W. Kincaid," he read. "From Endless Summer Resorts."

"Who's that?" Irwin asked.

Craig shrugged. "Never heard of them."

"I have," said Liz, thoughtfully. "But I can't remember where."

* * *

"Amber, wake up!" whispered Liz. She stood on her tiptoes and shook the sleeping figure in the top bunk.

"Elliot, you promised," groaned Amber. "No more drinks before bed."

"Not *that!* I just remembered where I've heard of Endless Summer Resorts before."

"Great, tell me in the morning," Amber mumbled. She plumped her pillow and rolled over.

"It is morning. Sort of." It was just before dawn, and everything outside was beginning to glimmer with a soft grey light. Liz tugged at Amber's arm. "Endless Summer Resorts has been trying to get hold of lakefront and recreational property."

"So, who cares?"

"My mother cares!" Liz persisted. "They're owned by a huge conglomerate. Last year Mom was at all kinds of special Real Estate Board

116

meetings because they tried to bulldoze some new zoning laws through city council. She says they come into a nice town like Ash Grove and buy up lakefront property any way they can. Then they build cheap, badly constructed condominiums, sell them, and get out."

Amber's eyes finally opened and she rolled over to face Liz. "So why would they be writing to Weird Walter?"

"I think we'd better find out."

"We need to see that letter," decided Amber, kicking off her blankets.

Liz grinned. "I've already got my whipped cream."

Amber looked at her suspiciously. "Whipped cream?"

"For defence." She shook the can. "Or maybe revenge. I saved it from our first night. This stuff is so rank, it'll rot your socks."

"Sounds lethal." Amber slipped off the bed. "Let's go."

"In our nightgowns?"

"There's no time to get dressed. Just take your jacket. We need to hit Weird Walter's office before dawn. He's always up and prowling around early."

"What if someone sees us?"

Amber grinned. "Tell 'em we got lost going to the can."

As quietly as possible, they grabbed their

jackets and shoes and crept across the bare floor of the cabin. Amber paused a moment by Jane's bunk to make sure that their cabinmate really was asleep and that her quiet snoring wasn't fake.

With great care, Liz let the screen door shut gently. The two girls sat on the damp steps to pull on their shoes.

"Ready?" Amber whispered. She patted the pocket of her jacket to make sure her army knife was still there.

"All set."

Together they sprinted across the dew-laden grass and down the dark path to the building that housed the dining hall, kitchen and Kincaid's office. Amber was heading straight for the front door when Liz caught her arm.

"The back way. It's less likely we'll be noticed."

"Good thinking." Amber changed direction and they hurried to the door leading to the kitchen. Amber quickly slipped the latch, while Liz slapped at the mosquitos whining around them.

"Ugh! Let's get inside."

They ran through the kitchen, into the dining hall, and over to the door of Kincaid's office. Amber tried the handle.

"Is it locked?"

"Rats, yes."

It took a few minutes, but Amber finally slid up the lock. Liz pulled open the door and flicked on the light.

"Start with the desk," suggested Liz. She rifled through a wire basket filled with bills, while Amber searched the drawers.

"Nothing much here."

"Same here," Liz said. "It's got to be in the filing cabinet."

Amber crossed the room and gave the top drawer a tug. "It's locked." She fiddled around with her knife and finally hooked the lock with the corkscrew. "Dad was right," she said as it opened. "I did need a corkscrew." The drawer was full of file folders.

"Look under *E* for Endless," Liz suggested.

Amber flipped through the files. "Nothing."

"He probably hid it. Try another drawer."

"Right."

Liz glanced towards the door. "We'd better find it quick. It's starting to get light outside."

The second drawer held files on all the counsellors and staff, but none on Endless Summer Resorts.

"If it's not in this one, I don't know where else to look," Amber said as she yanked open the bottom drawer. After a few moments of fruitless searching, she sat back on her heels.

"Wait a minute," exclaimed Liz. "I can see something sticking up at the back."

Amber reached behind the files and pulled out a grey coloured folder. It was tied tightly shut. She jumped to her feet and pulled off the cord. It was full of papers and letters.

"Eureka!" declared Amber, taking the top sheet. "This must be the letter he got yesterday."

She read it aloud:

Dear Mr. Kincaid,

We appreciate your efforts to acquire the Ash Lake Camp property on our behalf. Our architects are already working on plans based on the map you sent last week.

Please accept the enclosed check as a token of our esteem.

Yours truly,
John Preston
Vice-President
Endless Summer Resorts

"That snake!" exclaimed Liz.

"Of all the low-down, dirty, rotten deals," fumed Amber. "Kincaid's been sabotaging the camp!"

"And blaming Mrs. Dainty."

Amber waved the letter in the air. "Not any more. We're going to nail him with this letter."

"I'll take that, if you don't mind!" Weird Walter Kincaid stood in the doorway, eyes blazing with anger.

"Oh, no you don't," yelled Amber. "Zap him, Elliot!"

Liz aimed her can of whipped cream at the director and pressed frantically on the nozzle. A puff of rancid cream plopped to the floor. The rest drizzled down the side of the can into a smelly puddle at her feet.

"You pathetic brats," sneered Kincaid as he slapped the can from Liz's hands.

"Run for it!" Amber screamed.

The two girls dashed toward the door, but Kincaid easily intercepted them. "Oh, no you don't," he said, gripping each one painfully by the arm. "Let's go! You two won't be causing me any more trouble."

As he pulled them toward the door, Amber let the letter flutter to the floor. "Where are you taking us?" she demanded.

"To Skull Island." Kincaid grinned menacingly. "You've heard the legend, haven't you?"

11

Marooned on Skull Island

Liz and Amber stared in horror at the camp director.

"Let us go!" Amber demanded, jerking her elbow furiously. It was no use. He held their arms too tightly.

Weird Walter smiled, not very pleasantly.

"Sorry, girls. Your disappearance will be just a bit more bad news for Eastern Technology. And they hate bad news. But it will make the Board eager to sell the camp for the price my client is offering."

"You can't do that," Liz told him hotly. "The city council voted against zoning changes."

"Do you think a small-town city council is any

match for a big corporation?" Kincaid scoffed. "This camp already has the right zoning."

"Then we'll stop you!" Amber declared.

"Don't make me laugh." He pushed them out the door of his office. "Don't even think of trying to attract someone's attention." He patted the sheathed fishing knife hanging from his belt. "I don't want to have to do something unpleasant to you, but I will. There's just too much money at stake."

"N-no," Liz stammered.

Kincaid frog-marched them through the dining room and across the deserted camp. The girls looked frantically for someone, anyone, to rescue them. No one was around. The morning mist curled eerily across the lake as Weird Walter hustled them down the dock to the motorboat.

"You can't get away with this," Amber told him furiously. "They'll know you sabotaged the camp."

"It doesn't matter any more. Besides, it was Bennie. He'll do anything for money, including a little arson," Kincaid chuckled. "Into the boat."

Liz, then Amber, reluctantly stepped down into the damp hull. Without taking his eyes off them, Kincaid untied the boat. "You two have been so much trouble, I'm actually going to enjoy this." He leaned over and grabbed the rope mooring the adjacent canoe to the dock.

"What's the canoe for?" demanded Amber.

Kincaid smiled cruelly. "A couple of missing campers, an overturned canoe drifting out on the lake . . . "

"Everyone will think we've drowned!" exclaimed Liz.

"You got it."

"You'll go to jail for this!" sputtered Amber.

"By the time anyone figures out what's happened, I'll be in Brazil," he bragged. "I've got everything I need — plane tickets, passport, money. As soon as I dump you, I'm out of here. Eastern Technology will be forced to close down the camp."

He jumped lightly into the boat, still clutching the canoe's mooring line, then pointed to the seats at the back by the motor. "You two sit there. And don't try to jump out. This motor has eighty horsepower — the propeller could do very nasty things to you."

"Wouldn't dream of it," Amber said, backing over to her seat.

Weird Walter stood at the front and started the engine. The noise echoed across the lake.

"Now what?" Liz whispered as they pulled away from the dock, the canoe dragging alongside.

Amber didn't answer. She was biting her lip, staring straight ahead at Kincaid's back as he steered the boat. Liz watched in fascination as

Amber's hand slowly moved up and down over the back of the boat.

"Amber?"

"Ssh."

Halfway across the lake, Kincaid abruptly cut the engine. "This is where you get off."

"No!" screeched the girls in unison.

Kincaid laughed. "No," he decided. "Tempting as it is, I'll take you a little closer to shore. But first . . . " He bent over the side and rocked the canoe.

Amber lunged out of her seat. Kincaid was too quick for her. "Don't even think it," he snarled, forcing her back beside Liz, "or I'll change my mind and dump you here." Then he gave the canoe a hefty shove and the lightweight craft flipped over.

Kincaid gunned the engine once again. "Next stop, Skull Island."

The fog was thicker there, the trees rising like giant fingers through the mist. Kincaid put the boat in neutral as they neared shore.

"Get out," he said coldly.

"We're not at the shore," Liz protested.

"It's only a metre or so deep. You won't drown."

"Fat lot you'd care if we did," Amber said hotly.

"Get out or I throw you out," Kincaid growled.

Without another word, Amber and Liz hopped over the side of the boat. "This is freezing!" Liz gasped.

"You jerk!" Amber shouted behind her as she and Liz slogged through waist-high water towards the shore. Kincaid laughed, revved the motor, and sped away.

Liz climbed onto the beach, muttering furiously and ringing out the sopping skirt of her nightgown.

"Shut up, Elliot."

"But my sneakers are squelching!"

"Quiet!"

Reluctantly, Liz stopped and listened. All she could hear was the motorboat roaring . . . then spluttering . . . then silence on the lake. The cry of a loon and Weird Walter's curses drifted across the still water.

"What the —"

Amber grinned and sloshed up onto the beach. "It's really awesome what a corkscrew will do to a fuel line." She flourished her pocketknife.

"Ha!" Liz crowed. "Partner, you're brilliant!"

"Naturally."

Amber sat down and emptied her sneakers. Liz peered through the mist.

"I don't see the boat," she reported. "He must have gotten at least a third of the way. What if he paddles in from there?"

"He can't, remember? We took the spare paddle out of the motorboat after the other one got broken in the Great Race."

"That's right! Too bad there aren't any great white sharks out there."

"I'd even settle for nasty little brown ones," Amber replied.

Liz surveyed the empty beach. "Kincaid's not only criminal, he's irresponsible," she shivered. "We're soaking wet. We could die of pneumonia!"

"We have to get off this island somehow," Amber said determinedly. "And fast. Kincaid might still drift to shore. Or swim."

"I'll bet he's already sent in a full report of the camp's troubles to the Board of Directors at Eastern Technology."

"It's up to us to tell them the truth."

"But how?"

* * *

"Rise and shine!" Michelle called loudly.

Jane pulled the blanket over her head. She had been dreaming that Dobbs and Dexter, Inc. had racked up another million, and Amber and Liz were looking for a job . . .

"Get up, Jane."

"All right!"

Jane sat up and automatically checked the bunks Amber and Liz occupied. Both were empty.

"Hard to believe they were the first ones up," Annette commented as she pulled on a T-shirt.

"Weird," Cathy Daniels agreed.

"But they aren't dressed yet," Jane said.

"How do you know?" Michelle asked.

"Because Amber always half-stuffs her nightgown under her pillow," Jane replied. "It's not there."

They all looked at Amber's bunk. The covers were in a tangled heap and the pillow hung half over the side of the bed.

"Looks like Amber was in a hurry," Cathy laughed. "A quick sprint to the can."

"Probably," Jane agreed quickly. But if Amber and Liz were up to something, she wanted to know about it. After all, she was one of the partners in Dexter Enterprises.

Jane tucked in her T-shirt, ran a brush through her hair, then trotted out of the cabin towards the girls' bathroom. A few campers were brushing their teeth or taking showers, but there was no sign of either Amber or Liz.

"I knew it, they're up to something," she fumed.

At breakfast, Jane poked over her French toast. Craig, Jonathan and Irwin were eating and joking around with the boys from their cabin. One by one the campers finished and left the dining room. Jane lingered over the meal, keeping an eye on the door. Eventually, Amber and Liz would have to show up for breakfast. Then she would pounce.

"Not hungry this morning, dear?" Mrs. Dainty sat down beside her with her own breakfast.

"No, I was waiting for Amber and Liz. They didn't eat early, did they?"

Mrs. Dainty paused, searching her memory. "I don't think I saw them this morning. I guess they're just sleeping in. It's such a miserable morning, you can't blame them."

"No, I guess not."

She quickly finished her breakfast and went outside. For a moment, she paused in front of the dining hall, trying to decide what to do. The boys might know what Amber and Liz were up to, but she didn't want anyone to think that she cared. Jane frowned. She'd just look around the camp herself — casually.

It didn't take long to recheck the cabin and bathroom. Then Jane ran along the beach. The arts and crafts room was full, but Amber and Liz weren't among the campers.

"This is weird," Jane said to herself. Now her curiosity was really piqued. She'd have to check with the boys after all.

* * *

Craig, Irwin and Jonathan were staring intently at a computer screen, alternately making notes and keying in commands, when Jane burst into the computer room.

"Hey, Jane." Irwin beamed and waved her over.

"I think we've found the glitch, Mr. Sharkman," Craig called.

"Wonderful, boys." Mr. Sharkman watched the screen over their shoulders.

"Where are Amber and Liz?" Jane demanded.

"Who cares?" Craig replied, leaning over to key in another command.

"I haven't seen them this morning," Irwin answered. "Do you know where they are, Jonathan?"

"Nope."

"Is there a problem?" Jaws asked, peering at Jane over his glasses.

"I'm not sure, sir," she said. "They weren't in their beds this morning when we woke up, and nobody seems to have seen them since last night."

"What?"

"Are you serious?" Jonathan asked.

Jane nodded.

"I bet they're on the case," Craig declared. "They like skulking around in the middle of the night."

"What case?" Mr. Sharkman asked sharply.

"You know, sir," Craig said. "All the weird stuff that's been going on around here. Amber and Liz figure there's something fishy about it, and they've been investigating. But they haven't found anything yet."

"Except that prowler," Jonathan said suddenly.

"Prowler?" Jaws was obviously startled. "Amber and Liz saw a prowler? Did they report it to Mr. Kincaid?"

"Uh, no."

"Why not?" Jaws asked sternly.

"Actually, sir, we saw him with Mrs. Dainty," Jonathan said reluctantly. "We all thought if we said anything, it would get her into more trouble."

"And, like Amber says, there was no proof of anything," Irwin added. "I mean, it may be crazy, but there's no law against giving strangers money in the middle of the night."

"*Irwin!*"

Jaws frowned and stared into space. "Hmm. How strange — and how unlike Mrs. Dainty. Come along," he said abruptly. "We'd better report all of this to Mr. Kincaid."

"But he already's blaming Mrs. Dainty for the missing tuck shop money," Irwin protested.

"That's right, sir," Jane added.

"Amber and Liz appear to be missing," Jaws said firmly. "Mr. Kincaid, however irascible, is the camp director. He must be told about this so that a search can be started. I'm sure Mrs. Dainty can make her own explanations, if necessary. Let's go."

Reluctantly, Jonathan, Craig, Jane and Irwin followed Jaws to Kincaid's office off the dining room. Mr. Sharkman rapped sharply on the door. "Mr. Kincaid," he called. There was no answer.

"I don't think he's there," Mrs. Dainty spoke from her seat across the room. "His phone was ringing and ringing a few minutes ago."

"But the light's on," Jane said, noting the glow through the frosted glass window. "Honestly, for all his efficiency talk, he should at least switch off the light." She pushed open the door.

"Pheww!" Craig said. "What's that smell?"

"Gross!" Irwin added, holding his nose.

Together they went into the office.

"Something's spilled on the floor." Jane pointed to a whitish-yellow puddle.

"Smells like sour milk," Irwin said.

"And somebody dropped a letter into it." Jane leaned over to pick up the paper. "This is really too disgusting."

"Craig, look." Jonathan pointed to the can of whipped cream lying in the corner. "Liz had a can like that the other night."

"Then they must have been here," Craig said. "Mr. Sharkman, I think there really is something strange going on."

"You'd better look at this letter." Jane handed

the soggy sheet to Jaws. Her face was as white as the paper.

Mr. Sharkman read the letter, then read it again. The boys crowded close and looked over his shoulder.

"The girls must have found this," Craig said.

"And Kincaid must have found them," Jonathan finished, pointing to the puddle of sour cream.

"But where are they now?" Jaws said. He paused for only a moment. "Irwin, get your father on the line. Amber and Liz may need all the help we can get . . ."

12

Hook, Line and Sinker

The girls shivered on the rocky beach of Skull Island as they tried to figure out a way off. They stared alternately at the water and the misty trees.

"Amber, do you suppose there ever were two Indian princesses who disappeared here?" Liz asked.

"No, Kelly made that up."

"Then why do they call this Skull Island?"

Amber jumped up. "Elliot, you're getting morbid. We've got to do something. We're cold, we're wet, and that jerk is getting away."

Reluctantly, Liz got to her feet. "I don't think I can swim all the way back to camp — at least not in my nightgown and sneakers."

Amber giggled. "True. But there must be something we can do. Otherwise Kincaid will win."

"And probably Craig and Jonathan will end up rescuing us. That I can live without," Liz added.

"Okay," Amber said. "We know we're brilliant — now's the time to prove it. Let's see." She began pacing across the narrow beach, sneakers squooshing with every step. "We're stuck on this island."

"Haunted island," interjected Liz, taking another quick glance at the fog-shrouded trees.

"Deserted island," Amber said firmly. "And — "

"What did you say?"

"We're on a deserted island," Amber repeated patiently.

"No, we aren't," Liz declared.

"What? You're getting delirious, partner."

"Mrs. Dainty's prowler."

Amber stared. "You're right," she said slowly. "And he has a boat."

"He may be a blackmailer," Liz pointed out.

"Yes, but he has a boat."

"Do you expect me to walk up to a perfect stranger in my nightgown?" Liz demanded.

"Do you want Kincaid to close down the camp?"

Liz paused. "Maybe we could *borrow* the boat if he's not around," she suggested.

They thought for a moment. "It's our only chance," declared Amber.

Liz nodded and took a deep breath. "Okay, let's go for it."

They left the beach, heading towards the camp they had found the night they spent wandering around Skull Island. Before long, the girls were crouched in the bushes near the stranger's campsite.

A campfire burned invitingly and the smell of coffee hung in the air. The man they had seen in Mrs. Dainty's kitchen sat on a stump cleaning fish and whistling. A small motorboat was pulled up on a narrow strip of sand.

"Should we make a run for the boat?" Liz whispered.

Amber hesitated. "He doesn't look very big, but I'll bet we'd never make it. Maybe if we wait, he'll leave."

"And go where?" Liz demanded. "If he leaves, it'll be in the boat."

Amber shifted uncomfortably, breaking off a twig that was sticking in her ribs. "What about a diversion?"

"Sounds good," Liz said. "What've you got in mind?"

"Nothing. Can't you think of something?"

Liz pondered for a moment. "We could tell

him we were shipwrecked and our friend's hurt back on the beach."

"Even if he bought that one, he'd expect us to show him," Amber said.

"Maybe we could outrun him."

"But what if we can't?" Amber replied. They lapsed into silence. "We have to make a decision soon," she said. "Kincaid could be making it to shore by now."

Liz slowly twisted a strand of hair around her finger. "Amber," she said, "I think we should trust him."

"What? Are you crazy? We don't know anything about him."

"We know he was with Mrs. Dainty," Liz pointed out. "And we're sure she's innocent, especially after what Kincaid said. It seems logical that if she wasn't doing anything wrong when they were together, then he wasn't either."

Amber's eyes narrowed. "You're right," she said. "We thought he was a friend of hers in the first place, and good detectives always trust their gut instincts. Besides," she added, "I don't know what else to do. Let's go."

They stepped boldly out of the bushes and walked towards the stranger.

"Excuse me!" Amber said loudly.

"What!" The man twisted around, blue eyes opening wide. After a moment he smiled. "You girls scared me half to death."

Amber and Liz blushed furiously as he looked at their soggy outfits.

"I'll bet you two left your overnight camp and got lost," he went on, trying not to grin. He wiped his scaling knife on the grass, slipped it into the sheath at his belt, and stood up. "Funny, I didn't hear you kids coming in last night. Usually you campers make enough noise to wake up a ghost or two."

"We didn't come in last night," Liz told him.

"And we're not camping," Amber said. "We were marooned here."

"What?"

"We're from Eastern Technology's computer camp," Liz started to explain.

"That's right," Amber went on in a rush. "Weird Walter and his henchman, Bennie Somebody, are sabotaging the camp so the company will sell to a big resort chain. But we found out, so that creep Kincaid left us here on the island. And we've got to get back before he gets away, so we have to borrow your boat right now. *Please!*"

"Whoa," the stranger said. "Can you prove all this?" he demanded excitedly. "That's why I'm out here on the island — I'm trying to get the goods on Endless Summer Resorts."

Liz nodded. "That's the company. There's a letter from Endless Summer Resorts in Kincaid's office. He was behind all the trouble at camp.

Now he's been paid off and he's got plane tickets for Brazil."

"We've got to stop him! It's the only chance to get my marina back from that sleazy corporation!"

"What do you mean your marina?" demanded Amber.

"My wife Rose and I used to own the Ash Lake Marina."

"What?" Amber cried. "You mean Mrs. Dainty's your wife? We thought you were dead!"

"There's no time to go into that now. Kincaid could be halfway to the airport."

"I don't think so," said Liz. "We kind of slowed him down a bit."

Amber grinned. "I punched holes in his boat's fuel line, so he's drifting around out on the lake somewhere," she explained. "But we need to get to a phone and make sure ET understands that the camp is great."

"And call the police about Kincaid," Liz added.

Mr. Dainty nodded briskly. "After the bad time he's given Rose, that idea sounds real good. Let's go, girls."

In next to no time, Mr. Dainty had pushed the boat off the beach and Amber and Liz had clambered in. He gave the boat another good shove, then jumped in himself and gunned the outboard motor. This time Amber and Liz sat near the prow, wind streaming through their hair.

"Derelict ahoy!" Liz shouted suddenly. The fog had begun to lift, and there ahead of them was Kincaid's boat. The camp director stood up and waved both his arms.

"*Hi, there!*" he yelled. "*I'm having a little trouble with my motor. Could you —* " His words trailed off as he caught sight of Amber and Liz.

Mr. Dainty slowed the motor until the boat was barely moving. "Got a problem?" he called out.

"Yes, uh, yes." Kincaid's eyes narrowed as he stared at the two girls. "Amber, Liz!" he exclaimed suddenly. "I'm glad to see you're safe."

"*What?*"

"Glad you found these two," he went on, smiling widely at Mr. Dainty. "We've been looking for them since early this morning. They borrowed a canoe without permission. I was afraid something had happened to them."

"He's lying!" Amber shouted.

"Now, Amber," Kincaid said in an oily voice. He turned his attention to Mr. Dainty. "I'm afraid these two are the camp troublemakers. Always concocting wild stories. I'll bet they told you a good one."

"Matter of fact, they did," Mr. Dainty replied. "I don't know when I've heard such a fishy story, and I've heard quite a few."

"You don't believe *him*, do you?" Amber demanded.

"Mr. Dainty!" Liz said reproachfully.

"Dainty?" Kincaid repeated. His face suddenly whitened.

"That's right," the man replied. "Rose's husband. And the former owner of Ash Lake Marina."

"No, no," Kincaid stammered. "There must have been a mistake."

"That's right," Mr. Dainty said. "And you made it! Now I'm going to toss you a long rope to tie to your bow, and we'll tow you in."

"Don't do it," Amber said. "Leave him out here."

"We were hoping for sharks," Liz added.

Mr. Dainty laughed. "This one's a shark all right, but now that the fog's burning off, I believe I see a police car by the camp dock." Sure enough, a police car and a crowd of milling campers were clearly visible on shore.

"All right!" Amber declared.

Mr. Dainty knotted a line to the back of his boat and tossed the other end to Kincaid. The camp director scowled, but caught the rope and slowly tied it to the bow of his boat. As Mr. Dainty revved up his motor, Kincaid sat in the back of the boat, his head in his hands.

By the time they pulled into shore, half the campers were on the beach. Mr. Sharkman,

Detective Dexter, Irwin, Jane, Craig and Jonathan rushed out on the dock.

"Are you girls all right?" Mr. Sharkman asked anxiously.

"Of course," Amber declared as she jumped out of the boat. "Everything is completely under control."

"Mr. Dainty helped us," Liz added.

Detective Dexter nodded. "Good. It's a real relief that nothing's happened to you — "

"We have to hurry," Amber interrupted. "We've got to get hold of Craig's father. You won't believe what that creep Kincaid has been doing."

"Oh, yes, we would," Craig replied. "When Jane found out you were missing, we went to Kincaid's office and found the letter."

"And the whipped cream," Jonathan interjected.

"Jane noticed we were missing?" Amber asked dubiously.

"That's right," Irwin said proudly.

"You aren't the only ones who know how to do detective work, you know," Jane told them. "Mrs. Dainty and I also apprehended the tuck shop thief helping himself to a little getaway money." She pointed to a sullen-faced Bennie, handcuffed to the door handle of Detective Dexter's squad car.

"You should pay your employees better, Mr. Kincaid," Irwin shouted out. "Keeps them loyal."

"That's right, Kincaid," added Detective Dexter. "I'm looking forward to a lengthy chat with you after what Bennie's been telling me." He turned to Craig and Jonathan. "Okay, boys, let's reel him in."

Everyone looked out at the camp director's boat drifting at the end of Mr. Dainty's rope. Kincaid slumped down on his seat.

"Rule 13, subsection 4," Liz called out. *"There will be no boating without permission!"*

The crowd on the dock jeered and clapped wildly.

"And your boating privileges are hereby suspended," yelled Amber, "for about twenty years!"

Epilogue

"I can't believe our two weeks are over," Amber said as she stuffed the last of her dirty T-shirts into a duffle bag. She and Liz were the last two left in the cabin. "When's your dad coming for us?"

"An hour," Liz said, consulting her watch.

"This was the weirdest camp in the history of the world," Amber went on. She held up a spare sock. "This yours?"

"Nope. Save it to offer Jane on the first day of school."

Amber giggled. "That should put a quick end to a brief friendship."

Liz grinned. "She's not so bad. It was her idea that Mr. and Mrs. Dainty run the camp now that Kincaid's in jail."

Amber sighed. "I hate to admit it, Elliot, but you're right. With the double salary, they'll soon be able to refinance their marina. And all's well that ends well, even if Jane did have a hand in it."

"Hmmm . . ."

She glanced at Liz, who was sprawled on her bunk reading a pamphlet. "What's that?"

"Something my mother sent me. I just got around to looking at it." Liz held up the brochure. "It's for a Mystery Writers' Convention at Ash Manor."

"Ash Manor!" Amber's attention was caught. "That old place is haunted."

"No, it isn't. The city's turned it into a convention centre. Do you want to go?"

"You bet I do." Amber grinned. "That place is so spooky, Elliot, there has to be at least one ghost . . ."

"But, Amber, we don't believe in ghosts. Do we?"

When she's not writing or reading mystery novels, **Anne Stephenson** keeps busy raising two kids, teaching a writing class, attending conferences and workshops, skiing, playing squash and knitting. Whew! Somehow, she also finds time for her two cats — Marmalade and Peanut Butter.

Susan Brown loves to travel, and she has lived in such places as Ottawa, Toronto, Detroit, Seattle and New York. She currently makes her home in Washington State, along with "assorted livestock" — three children, two gerbils and one dog. She is a freelance writer.

These "partners in crime" began their collaboration with the first Amber and Elliot mystery, *The Mad Hacker*, and are currently working on a television version of the series.